GRANNY MAGIC

ELKA EVALDS

Chicken House

2 Palmer Street, Frome, Somerset BA11 1DS
www.chickenhousebooks.com

Text © Elka Evalds 2019
Illustrations © Teemu Juhani 2019

First published in Great Britain in 2019
Chicken House
2 Palmer Street
Frome, Somerset BA11 1DS
United Kingdom
www.chickenhousebooks.com

Cover and interior design by Helen Crawford-White
Cover and interior illustrations by Teemu Juhani
Typeset by Dorchester Typesetting Group Ltd
Printed and bound in Great Britain by CPI Group (UK) Ltd, Croydon CR0 4YY

The paper used in this Chicken House book is made
from wood grown in sustainable forests.

1 3 5 7 9 10 8 6 4 2

British Library Cataloguing in Publication data available.

PB ISBN 978-1-912626-19-9
eISBN 978-1-912626-65-6

*In memory of
Grandma-in-Connecticut
and Grandma Pie*

Will didn't know the jumper was magic at first. It seemed dead ordinary. It had a round neck, long sleeves and stripes the width of bicycle tyres in navy blue, battleship grey and racing green. The only odd thing was a stripe near the bottom, which had bits of sparkly gold running through it. But only if you looked hard.

'Would you like something to help you remember Gran by?' Mum asked. 'You can pick anything you like.'

They were at Gran's house. All of her cupboard doors were open, and her belongings were heaped in piles. There were flower-covered dresses and flower-covered handbags and flower-covered rain hats. There were teapots shaped like cottages, and sugar bowls shaped like cabbages, and plates with pictures of the Isle of Man on them. And, of course, there were great honking hills of knitting.

Gran had knitted pincushions, tea cosies and shawls. She'd knitted coats for dogs, cases for glasses and hats for dolls. She'd knitted bathing costumes, dressing gowns and opera capes. She'd even knitted an umbrella once. If you'd asked Will if he'd like to have any of these things while Gran was still alive, he'd have said, 'Not bothered, thanks.' Will wasn't sure why it was different now that Gran had died.

The jumper lay on top of a mountain of mittens that Mum had poured on to Gran's kitchen table. With its arms spread wide, it looked as if it wanted to hug him. Will wasn't always keen on being hugged, but the jumper reminded him of things he'd forgotten, like coming to Gran's after school, back before there was rugby and Scouts. He'd helped her make chutney and pickles and jam. He'd built cities out of saucepans and spindles while Gran told him stories.

'That'll be too small for you, Bilbo,' Mum said when he reached for the jumper. But Will wouldn't let go of it. Instead, he put it on. 'Look! It fits!' he said. It was surprisingly soft.

'How funny!' said Mum, her eyebrows flying up. 'It's absolutely perfect.'

Suddenly Will felt much, much better. In fact, he felt downright happy.

'Can I pick something for Sophie?' he asked. Sophie was his little sister, who was five. 'Maybe there's a dog.' More than anything else in the world, Sophie loved dogs.

'You're very thoughtful all of a sudden,' said Mum, stroking his hair. They found a knitted corgi with a green pom-pom for a nose, then started home for lunch.

Will's house was on the other side of the river that ran through the middle of Knittington. He always went to Gran's by the wooden footbridge hidden between the old mills lining the banks. It wasn't really a shortcut, but it felt more secret than going over the stone bridge with the cars, and it smelt of ferns and wet stones.

As they stepped through the daisies in the

cracked car park though, a rumble erupted from the first of the big stone buildings. A cloud of dust puffed out of the open door.

'Oh look!' said Mum, stopping to see. 'Someone's fixing up that old woollen mill.'

There were vans parked next to the building, full of drills and screws and clamps. Coils of thick orange electrical cord spilt out of them. A lorry packed with crates and boxes stood open at the back. Wedged in the middle of the crates, Will could see a wire cage, with pointed pink noses poking in and out between the bars, twitching in the warm air.

'Are those weasels in that cage?' Will asked.

'Ferrets, I think,' said Mum. 'People use them to sniff out rats in old buildings.'

They came around the building towards the river, but yellow tape barred the path to the footbridge. NO TRESPASSING, read the signs, and BUILDING WORKS.

'But the new owner doesn't own the river too,' said Will, 'do they?'

'No,' said Mum, 'though they might be allowed to use the water for power.'

The building rumbled again and there was a blast of sound, like a hundred showers turning on at once. It drowned out the mossy rush of the river.

They had to retrace their path through the car park and then cross the river on the stone bridge. Will looked back down at the old mill as he and Mum climbed the cobbled street on the other side. The tall trees that grew along the riverbank blocked the view, but a breeze parted the branches for a second. Was that a face in the top-floor window? Ghost-white, it was looking down at the rushing water. Then the leaves hid the building again.

'I wonder what they're going to make in that old factory,' said Mum. 'Probably not jumpers and woolly hats any more.'

'Is that what they used to make?'

'A long time ago,' said Mum. 'It'll be good for Knittington to have something made here again, whatever it is.'

'Unless it's asbestos,' said Will, who liked logic. 'Or poison. Or nuclear waste.'

Mum smiled. 'Don't worry,' she said. 'But the town won't let anything harmful be made here.'

'I'm just saying,' said Will. 'Not *everything* would be good.'

2

*D*ing-dong! The doorbell rang while they were eating dinner.

'Oh pants!' said Will as Mum went to the door. 'Somebody's probably brought more pond slime.' Someone on Mumsnet had posted that the best thing to do for people who'd lost a loved one was to bring them healthy food. All of their neighbours must have read that post, because for two weeks now they'd been leaving beetroot casserole and soybean stew on the doorstep. Yesterday, Will had stuck his finger into a bowl of what looked like peanut butter icing but turned out to be extra-garlic hummus.

Sophie giggled. 'Pond slime!'

'With a side of lawn trimmings!' said Will.

Sophie laughed harder, kicking her legs under the table. 'And old tennis balls boiled in—'

'Will,' said Dad, 'our neighbours are being very kind, bringing us all of this food.' But he was smiling just a little bit as he said it.

Mum's face poked through the kitchen doorway. 'Some ladies who knew your mum,' she said to Dad.

'Eat three bites of those lawn trimmings, you two,' Dad said, following Mum out of the kitchen.

Will ate the three smallest shards of kale on his plate then went out to the hall. Mum and Dad were at the front door. Beyond them five old ladies were standing on the path. The smallest one was at the front. She had short, grey hair and gazed steadily through purple glasses. She stood up so straight that she *seemed* tall. The others crowded behind her. Each one of them was carrying a little china plate.

'This must be Will,' said Purple Glasses. She had a voice like a head teacher's.

'Yes,' said Dad. 'Our son.'

'Would you like to come in?' said Mum.

They filed in through the hall in order of height: first Purple Glasses; then a tiny little sparrow-lady whose cotton-wool hair was pulled up into a bun on the top of her head; next a willowy one with two silver plaits and a flowery tunic; then a stout one with strong arms and a man's hat, and finally a tall one with owlish glasses and a startled expression.

They said they were Gran's knitting club.

'Her knitting club?' asked Dad, glancing at Mum as she came into the living room with a tea tray. 'I didn't know Mum had a knitting club – I thought she just knitted on her own.'

'Not that it's surprising!' Mum chuckled. 'It's just that we never heard her talk about you.'

'Not much to tell, really,' said the one with the purple glasses.

'A bunch of old ladies sitting around knitting baby booties,' said the tall one, blinking mildly behind her round glasses.

Will didn't mind if they were Dracula's aunties. They'd brought butterscotch biscuits, lardy-cake wedges, hazelnut brownies, caramel toffee and honeycomb flapjacks. But he couldn't help noticing that their eyes went all around the house while they drank their tea, as if they were searching for something. At some point, each one of them noticed the knitted cushions on the sofa, and then nodded at one of the others. When Sophie climbed down from Dad's lap they spotted the knitted dog's head sticking out from her pocket, and the tall one asked if she could hold 'that dear little puppy'.

'She's a corgi,' said Sophie, 'and her name is Omelette and she can get big to fight thieves.'

Did Will just imagine it, or did all of the ladies lean forward to look as the tall one held the little dog up, turning it over and over in the light?

'. . . and so we wondered if any of Gertie's patterns might be left – or half-finished projects, or anything at all that she knitted, really,' Purple Glasses was saying. Gertie was Gran.

'We'd dearly love to have any of it, if it's going begging,' said the one with the man's hat.

'Oh, if only I'd known!' said Mum. 'There were bags and bags, but it all went to the charity shop, just this afternoon.'

'Oh!' said the sparrow-lady softly, as if something had hurt her.

'I'm so sorry,' said Mum.

'Don't fret,' said the owlish one, patting Mum's hand.

'But if anything else turns up, and you'd like it off your hands, we'd greatly appreciate it if you'd let us come and get it,' said Purple Glasses, putting her cup down and heading for the door, followed by the other old ladies. 'You can find us at the knitting shop in Woolwick Lane.'

'How mysterious!' said Mum, as she shut the door. 'All this time they were knitting together, and I'd never even heard their names before.'

'I always said there was more to my mum than met the eye,' said Dad. Will couldn't tell if he was joking.

Ding-dong.

Will was cleaning his teeth and Sophie was choosing bedtime stories when the doorbell rang again. Will rinsed his toothbrush, then followed the voices back downstairs to the living room.

On the sofa sat a small man wearing a neat suit, with a stripy jumper underneath. He had a tiny sharp nose, an egg-smooth forehead, and eyebrows like white wolf tails. There was a large box of chocolates on the table beside him. *Epic!* thought Will, then peeped down at the box and saw it was Turkish Delight. *Yuk.*

'I want to offer my deepest condolences,'

the man was saying. His voice was smooth but reedy, like an oboe.

Something moving caught Will's eye and he glanced up from the table. *Weird!* For a second he thought the stripes on the man's jumper had started waving, like octopus arms. But now he was looking directly at them, he could see that the stripes were still. They were just diagonal, knitted in a kind of spiral . . . Will stepped closer to get a better look.

'Ah! Here's our son, Will,' Dad said. 'Will, come and meet Mr Fitchet. He used to know Gran.'

'Hello,' said Will.

'Hello, young man.' Mr Fitchet turned towards Will and put his hand out to shake. He had a pressed-thin grin. Will stretched his hand out, and Mr Fitchet clamped it softly with both of his, keeping Will close while peering into his face. He had the brightest blue eyes Will had ever seen, and they looked at him without blinking.

'I'll bet you're a clever one,' he said, letting go of Will's hand suddenly, as if he'd been burnt. 'Like your grandad.' His smile fell, like a marble dropping off the edge of a table.

'And here's our daughter,' said Mum, as Sophie came running into the room. 'Come and say hello to Mr Fitchet, Sophie.'

Sophie leant up against Mum's legs shyly, and Mr Fitchet bent forward with his hands clasped. 'Ahh!' he said. 'This one looks like her gran!'

'Do you have a dog?' asked Sophie.

'No,' said Mr Fitchet, smiling his pressed little grin. 'I have some ferrets, though.'

'We saw ferrets in the back of a lorry today!' said Will. 'Down at the mills.'

Mr Fitchet peered at Will from under his wolf-tail eyebrows. 'Well observed, lad,' he said. 'I am now the owner of the old Woolman Mill, as it happens. So you probably saw my pets.'

Mum's face lit up. 'You'll have good neighbours,' she said. 'One of the other old factories has been fixed up with craft work-shops. There's a blacksmith, and some wood turners and candlemakers, and I think there's a potter now too.' Mum used to be an art teacher. She liked crafts.

'Is that the sort of thing you'll be putting into your building?' asked Dad.

'I had something bigger in mind,' said Mr Fitchet. He was stroking the sofa cushion. The one Gran had knitted.

'Well, we'll look forward to seeing what that might be,' said Dad.

'I wonder if I might confess something,' said Mr Fitchet, looking at the cushion under his hand. 'When I left Knittington as a young man, I hadn't a penny to my name. I've lived in many different cities over the years, and so I've had very few possessions. Now that I'm back again, it would mean a great deal to me to have something to help me remember Gertie.'

'Oh, I think that would be OK,' said Dad. 'The house is full of things Mum made.'

'That's really sweet,' said Mum.

'Would you like that cushion?' said Dad. 'The one you're holding?'

'No!' somebody squeaked. Will realized it was him. 'I mean – it's just . . .' His heart was pounding suddenly. 'That cushion has *always* been there. That's where it *belongs*.' He looked from Mum to Dad and back again. His face was burning with embarrassment, but he couldn't stop. 'We make forts out of those. We *need* them. All.'

Mum looked at Will and her eyes got shiny. 'Mr Fitchet, I'm very sorry but—'

The man put his hand in the air. 'Say no more, Mrs Shepherd,' he said.

'It's just—' Mum started again.

Mr Fitchet took both of Mum's hands in his, and smiled his little smile, looking at her from under his white eyebrows. 'I wouldn't hear of it, madam. Not another word, now.'

Will watched as Dad walked their guest to the front door, and the two stood next to the long table in the hallway, talking about the historic water turbine at the factory. (Why did grown-ups always take so long to say goodbye?) Then, just as Dad turned to open the door, Mr Fitchet's hand shot down, quick as a lizard's tongue, into the big basket where Dad and Mum left keys and pens and phones, and put something in his pocket. It happened so quickly that Will wasn't sure it had.

'What a sweet man,' said Mum, back in the kitchen as the front door closed.

'I saw him put something in his pocket!' Will said. 'Something from the basket in the hall.'

'Are you sure?' said Mum, looking at him with her head tilted. 'What did you think it was?'

But Will didn't know.

'I think you must have made a mistake, Will,' said Dad. 'Why would he do that?'

Will didn't know that either.

3

Dad was in the study and Mum was in the bathroom when Sophie started crying the next morning.

'What's the matter, Soph?' Will asked.

'I can't find m-my n-new juckie!' Juckie was Sophie's word for dog.

Will sat down on the floor next to her. She was surrounded by dogs: wooden dogs, plastic dogs, even a chipped china dog – and of course all the knitted dogs Gran had made.

'The corgi we brought you yesterday?' asked Will.

Sophie nodded. 'I put it in the basket. In the hall.'

So *that* was what Mr Fitchet had put into his pocket! Will hadn't imagined it.

Sophie's tears ran down her cheeks and she began to breathe in little gasps. Will knew these gasps. They would build up and up and up, until she finally let out a World-Cup Wail. Sophie could have wailed for England.

'Hey!' he cried. 'Want to wear my jumper?' Will pulled the jumper off quickly. 'Because Gran made it.' He scrunched it up and looped the neck hole over Sophie's head. She tugged at it wildly for a second, and then suddenly stopped. 'So it's sort of like Gran's hugging you when you wear it.' Sophie *did* like being hugged.

She gasped twice and then let out a long sigh.

Phew! thought Will. He pulled Sophie's arms through the jumper's sleeves.

'And see how there's one stripe with golden sparkles in it?' he asked. 'It's . . . fairy dust!' Sophie loved that kind of stuff.

Sophie traced the odd stripe with her finger

silently for a minute. Then she looked up and smiled.

'Let's make it quiet for Dad,' she said. Dad was having trouble concentrating. He worked at the local museum, and today he was writing a special lecture for the big Open Day at the end of August. 'Let's wrap up the house in earmuffs.'

'Hmm,' said Will. 'How about some pillows and blankets around the study door instead?'

The study was really just a cupboard with a tiny table and chair in it, and it didn't take very long to build a wall of blankets and pillows in front of the door. (*Ha*, thought Will. *We DO need all of these sofa cushions.*) But then Dad opened the door.

'What are you two—?' He watched the pile of cushions skid across the floor.

'Shhh,' said Sophie. 'We're making it quiet.'

'Oh, is *that* it?' said Dad. For a second he closed his eyes and looked like he was trying not to laugh. 'That is very, very thoughtful of you, Sophie.' He crouched down. 'But the real noise isn't out here,' he said gently. 'It's in here.' He tapped the side of his head.

'Come on, you two,' said Mum from behind them. 'Let's leave Dad in peace.' She patted their backs and led them into the kitchen. 'Is that the jumper you took from Gran's?'

'Yep,' said Will, running to get the bowls out for breakfast.

'I *thought* it was too small for you,' said Mum. 'Look how it fits Sophie.'

Will felt his mouth drop open as he looked at Sophie. The jumper fitted her perfectly. But Sophie was only five, and little, like Gran had been. Will was nine, and tall, like Dad.

There was *definitely* something odd about that jumper.

He got it back when Mum took Sophie to karate. It was a bit of a squeeze pulling it over his head, but the sleeves seemed to grow as he pushed his arms through. The bottom did the same when he tugged it down over his stomach. It was like it was knitting itself as he pulled it on. The happy feeling poured into him again, like hot cocoa on a cold day.

'Are you sure you don't want to come with us, Will?' Mum called up the stairs.

'No, thanks,' said Will, looking around him. It was like he was seeing his own house for the first time. 'I have – um – stuff to do!'

It wasn't hard to find things that Gran had made. Wherever there were funny, bright colour combinations – red and purple spots on a lime-green background, say – and wherever things were made to look like something else – the tea cosy that was also an elf house, for instance – there was Gran.

Most of them, like Mum's patchwork cardigan or Sophie's Kitty Hat, seemed pretty ordinary when Will tested them. If they did anything special, Will couldn't work it out. But some of the things he found were different. They did their jobs with extra strength. A pair of Mum's mittens kept his hands electric-warm even when he held a bag of frozen peas for ten minutes. A knitted flannel under the bathroom sink cleaned the grass stains from his jeans without any soap or water or anything.

And two of the knitted things were down-right *cosmic*.

The first was a pair of Dad's socks with multi-coloured stripes and sparkly gold heels that Will found in the bottom of the laundry basket. Would they keep his feet extra warm? he wondered. He started towards the freezer to fetch the frozen peas again, and a strange thing happened. It was as if something was pushing him, gently, behind his ankles. His steps came out extra long. *Weird*.

He tried jumping.

'Wow!' It was like there were tiny engines under his feet. How had Dad not noticed this? He could jump a good three centimetres higher wearing these socks! But then again, when did grown-ups ever jump?

Then there was the loo-roll cover on the

back of the toilet. It was knitted to look like a Dalek. Will tried putting it on his head. 'Exterminate!' he said, turning his head round the bathroom. Nothing happened.

Hmmm, he thought. *If I were Gran, what power would I give to a loo-roll cover?*

It was then that he remembered his sheep. Gran had made it to put in his pocket, back when he first went to school. She had said that if he squeezed it, it would give him courage. Where was it now?

He went to his room and looked under his pillow, in his Lego box, and in the pocket of his winter coat.

'Where. Is. That. Sheep?' he asked out loud.

As soon as he finished saying this he was startled

by a tugging at the front of his eyeballs. It was as if his eyes were made of iron, and the bottom drawer of his desk was a magnet. His head followed his eyes, and his body followed his head, until he was sitting just in front of the desk, his heart pounding. He pulled the drawer open. Sliding his hand in, he felt his way back. Plastic dinosaurs. A cricket ball. Felt-tip pens. Back, further, lower. Something soft.

He wiggled it out. His sheep!

Just as he remembered, it had four horns, because of course Gran wouldn't make a regular old two-horned sheep. It was the colour of walnut coffee cake, and when he held it up in the sunlight, it sparkled with gold.

Will laughed out loud. What was going on? Was this something to do with the toilet-roll cover he was wearing on his head?

He tried the same trick with his dinosaur pencil, the missing tin opener, and Dad's Victorian penny that had been lost since

Easter. It worked every time. All he had to do was ask the question, then let his face follow his eyeballs, and walk towards wherever he was looking. Only when Will asked where he might find a suitcase full of banknotes and a skateboard did it stop working.

'Where is Sophie's knitted corgi?' he asked finally.

Will waited. The now-familiar tug pulled his eyeballs towards the stairs. His face and his legs came after. Down to the kitchen he went, following the pull, over to the boot room, through the swamp of wellies, and right up to the back door. He stopped for just a minute to ask himself if he was really brave enough to leave the house wearing a loo-roll cover on his head, and then ducked outside into the back garden.

Next door, Arthur and Rosie were weeding their striped flowerbeds. All of their flowers were striped, and some of the leaves. They liked to wear stripes too.

'Hello, Will! Like to come have a look at the

tiger rose? It's just come out!'

'Sorry! Can't stop!' said Will. His eyes were pulling him towards the back gate.

Next door on the other side, the Pingles were working on their latest invention: a trebuchet, which was an ancient kind of catapult, taller than Dad.

'Nearly ready to fire, Will!' said David. 'Want to give it a go?'

'Another time!' said Will, unlatching the gate and slipping through.

'Like to help fill the bird feeders, Will?' Miss Violet called from across the alley. She was president of the Knittington Bird Club, and had about a hundred different bird feeders.

'Not just now, thanks!'

'Nice hat, Will!' Olive and Annie's heads were bobbing up and down over their back fence. They were on pogo sticks. 'Come and race with us!'

'Sorry! Gotta run!'

Down the alley, over the road, across the abbey cloister, and out on to the high street

Will went. Then suddenly his eyeballs stopped outside a shop. He blinked and stared. A puffy chair sat in the window, and next to it a shelf full of old teacups and a mannequin in a spotted summer dress with a floppy straw hat on its head. Why would the loo-roll cover have brought him to a shop in the high street when he had asked to find Sophie's dog?

He looked again. Actually, the hat wasn't straw at all. It was knitted. It had stripes of mint green, royal blue, cherry red and, along the edge . . . sparkling gold.

Will stepped back to look at the sign above the window. Oxfam. This must be where Mum had brought the bags from Gran's flat. This shop might be full of Gran's knitting! There might be more high-jumping socks or who-knew-what fun in there!

Will whipped the loo-roll cover off his head, stuffed it into his pocket, and pushed the door open.

4

The shop smelt like dust, strong laundry soap and old-fashioned mothballs. There were shelves with shoes and hats, shelves with lampshades and saucepans, and shelves with puzzles and games. Tall metal racks were hung with jackets and dresses and jeans and pyjamas and coats.

A lady in a blue pinny was bending down behind the front counter, arranging china hedgehogs under the glass. As Will stepped up to ask about the hat, something sparkled on the counter top. It was a shoe box full of mittens. Carefully, so no one would tell him off for making a mess, he stirred through the box. Yellow with purple, turquoise with olive, pink with red and orange. Definitely made by Gran! There was even one like his jumper: battleship grey and navy blue, with golden speckles running through one of the stripes.

'I'd like to buy this box of mittens, please,' he said. 'How much are they?'

'Oh,' the lady laughed, 'I should think you could have them all for a pound. You see, they're all singles. None of them match.'

'That's OK,' Will said, pulling a pound coin from his pocket.

'There's been quite a run on hand-knitted things today,' said the lady, as she took the coin. 'I've never seen woolly items sell so well in July!'

'Perhaps everyone is planning ahead.'

Will didn't have to turn around. He knew that smooth-oboe voice – it was Mr Fitchet. So he was right! Mr Fitchet must have Sophie's dog. *That* was why the knitted hat had brought him here.

'I had my eye on that box myself.' He

stepped forward, next to Will. 'You see, I'm always losing my mittens,' he said, looking under his wolf-tail eyebrows at Will. 'If all my mittens were mismatched to start with, I wouldn't have to worry.'

Will tried to speak, but when he opened his mouth, no sound came out.

'I'd be prepared to pay ten pounds for that box of mittens,' the man went on, turning to the counter with a stiff ten-pound note in his hand. The lady in the pinny looked very surprised.

'Stop! Wait!' Will burst out. 'I have ten pounds too! Or, at least, I think I might have nearly seven. I'd *very* much like to buy these mittens, please,' he said to the lady. 'My gran knitted them, you see. Only she's dead now.'

'Bless the boy!' said the lady, putting her hand over her heart. 'Of course you can have them.'

Mr Fitchet's jaw twitched and his bright eyes seemed to simmer, like tiny pots of boiling oil. Will's mouth went dry. He wrapped his arms round the shoe box and slid it off the counter.

'Cheerio!' said the lady, bending back down to the china hedgehogs.

Will turned towards the door but, quick as a wink, Fitchet slithered in front of him, blocking the exit.

'I see you have a head for business, Will Shepherd,' he said softly. He looked Will up and down, his little grin widening slightly. 'What's your price then, boy?' He opened his wallet so Will could see the stack of twenty-pound notes inside.

Will's hands had gone sweaty and his legs felt like they'd just pedalled all the way up the hill to Gran's. But he stood up straight and raised his chin high.

'My sister's dog,' said Will, finding his voice. 'She was crying for it this morning. I know you have it.'

Mr Fitchet chuckled.

'I'm sorry to hear that,' he said. 'But I don't know why I'd need a woolly dog.'

'I don't know either,' said Will, forcing himself to speak slowly and calmly. 'And I don't know why you'd want these mittens or our cushion or anything else, but I *do* know that Gran wouldn't want you to steal her things.'

Mr Fitchet's skin turned spook-white. He bent down and put his pointy little nose up to Will's face.

'You just might be clever enough to figure it all out, Will Shepherd,' he said. 'But you will not be clever enough to stop me.'

5

Will ran all the way home. Only after he'd shut the back gate behind him did his hands relax around the shoe box. He took a deep breath, smelling the minty scent of Mum's herb garden. His heart went from gallop to canter to trot to walk.

But what in Gran's name was going on?

'What did you get up to today, Will?' asked Dad over their tofu-cabbage stew at dinner.

'Looking at some things Gran made,' Will said. Should he tell them? He hated it when *they* kept things from *him*. 'Did you know that the knitted flannel in the bathroom can clean practically anything?' he said. 'I think it might have special powers.'

Mum stared at him as if she were looking for signs of tropical plague. Then she laughed. Very hard.

'Well, if it's got you interested in cleaning I'd say it's definitely magical.'

No, Will thought. Grown-ups couldn't handle magic. They would think there was something wrong with him if he tried to make them believe it. And he didn't know *what* to say about Mr Fitchet.

'You really miss Gran, don't you?' Mum asked, squeezing his hand.

'Actually, yes,' said Will.

'Cronk does too,' said Sophie. Cronk was Gran's cat, who lived with them now. Cats did not rate as highly as dogs in Sophie's world, but they ran a close second. 'He's sad we can't go on holiday.'

'I'm sorry about that,' said Mum. They'd been planning to go on holiday with Gran this year. 'But at least we'll be here for the fete.'

They talked about the fete, and then Will asked, 'Did Gran always knit?'

'I think she was born knitting,' said Dad. 'She won a Blue Peter award when she was younger than you, knitting for the Seafarer's Fund. In fact, she met Grandad at a charity knit-a-thon.'

'*Grandad* used to knit?' asked Will. 'I thought he was a mechanic at the motorbike factory.'

'He was,' said Dad. 'And he played the fiddle, and he was a huge knitter. Lots of country people used to knit then, and sailors and fishermen too.' Dad still had Grandad's fiddle, and played in a folk band.

'But who taught her to knit?'

'Well, it wouldn't have been her own mum – my grandmum, that is. She was more of a cook than a knitter. But Gran's *gran* used to knit bandages for soldiers in both of the World Wars. She probably taught Gran.'

Will's head was spinning.

'It seems to skip generations,' said Mum. 'Like being left-handed.'

'I'm left-handed,' said Will.

'Yes, that's right,' said Dad. 'Skiffy. Just like Gran.'

'Perhaps he has *the gift*!' said Mum.

'What gift?'

'I'm only joking!' Mum laughed. 'It *was* special, though, Gran's knitting,'

'That's one way of putting it,' said Dad.

Mum smiled. 'OK, yes, it was crazy-looking. You couldn't wear half of it outside of the house. But I remember how she made me a knitted rabbit to take to the hospital when I had Will. I was supposed to squeeze it for the pain.'

'You swore it worked too!' said Dad. 'And she made me a little knitted lion to take to school in my pocket, to squeeze whenever I felt shy.'

Will nearly dropped his fork. That was just like his sheep.

Suddenly Mum stood up and started clearing plates. 'Who wants a butterscotch biscuit?' she said. But there was a tiny teardrop at the top of her cheek.

Will tried on one of the mittens before he got into bed. It didn't feel any different from any other mitten, but that meant nothing. He put the box on his desk and got under the covers. Tomorrow he'd figure out if the mittens did anything special. He smiled as his head hit the pillow. Maybe this summer, which had started off so sadly, would turn out to be fun after all.

6

Will woke in the darkness. Something had slithered or slid or very softly clicked. He opened his eyes. His furniture made black shapes in the grey air. Nothing moved except his curtains in the night breeze, filmy and colourless. A slice of moon showed him the outlines of the window, open much wider than when he'd gone to sleep.

There was no sound except his pounding heart. But a shape was moving. Something dark was scurrying across his floor. And something smelt like wet, dirty socks.

Will couldn't move a finger.

It looked like a cat. A slithering, loping cat.

Then it stood upright, like a fur-covered snake with tiny hands. It had something in its mouth.

There was more than one. They were all over the floor.

Will opened his mouth to shout, but no sound came out. One of the shapes jumped up to the windowsill, silhouetted in the street lamp, and in less than a second it had disappeared, with nothing but the smallest rustle of sound. One by one, just as quietly, the others flowed out of the window, each with something in its mouth.

Like a ball released from a ruck, Will found he could move again.

He shot out of bed and over to the window. The strange humpbacked things were loping across the back garden in the moonlight. *Ferrets!* With mittens in their mouths!

Will whipped his head round. The shoe box lay empty on the floor.

He pulled on his magic jumper, and

courage rushed into him like oil into an engine. He tied on his trainers and, almost as silently as the thieving ferrets, ran down the stairs and out through the back door. His bike was leaning up against the shed. Will pushed it quickly into the alley, and looked up and down for the ferrets. There! Off to the right!

Never had Will pedalled so fast, not even when he and Ben had crashed a cricket ball

into Rafi's brother's bike. Around the corner he pedalled, following the bobbing tails and humping backs, across the marketplace, and over the paving stones of the ruined abbey cloister. The ferrets flitted round corners, under fences and over curbs, but Will knew all the twists and turns of Knittington.

Down the hill towards the river the ferrets flew, and then over the little bridge, turning sharply into the trees along the riverbank.

Will sped after, ducking through the wet branches, twigs cracking below. He could just make out the furry humps of the ferrets bobbing through the ferns, mittens in their mouths. They were heading for the back of the Woolman factory. Will let his bike fall on to its side and ran to the building, just in time to see the ferrets dive through a cat flap in a wide wooden door.

Creeping up to one of the yellow-lit windows, Will peered in to the basement of the factory. A row of iron columns ran down the centre of the stone floor, supporting a ceiling of thick wooden beams. Lined up in two rows on either side of the columns were steel machines on splayed legs, looking like giant spiders. Steel circles hung in the air above them, fitted with spools of coloured yarn. In the midst of them crouched Mr Fitchet, the ferrets streaming towards him, and jumping up on to his legs. As he took the mittens from their mouths, he gave each animal a treat.

So Fitchet had sent them on purpose to get into Will's house.

Suddenly Will became conscious of the fact that he was wearing his pyjamas and very far from his own bed. The darkness seemed very dark.

Inside, Fitchet spread the mittens on a steel table and picked up the one that looked like Will's jumper. He stretched it over a chrome stand and then pulled on a pair of glasses that looked like two brass microscopes. Making notes on a tablet beside him, he examined the mitten, and took pictures of it. Then, using a pair of tweezers, he slowly pulled a strand of sparkling gold yarn from the mitten, placed it on the table and separated it into three smaller strands.

Finally, Mr Fitchet walked over to one of the huge spider machines and pressed a button on it. A screen lit up on one side of it, and the man began typing on a keyboard. He did the same at two other machines. A deep thrumming shook the building, and Will felt his palm tremble on the window ledge. The man took the thin strands of sparkling wool and fed them, one by one, into the machines.

The thrumming grew louder. Then, *clickety clackety slap clack crash,* the machines began to whirl, the coloured spools to spin. Ten seconds later, each of the machines spat what looked like a mitten on to the floor. Mr Fitchet scooped the mittens up, and spread them on the table under the lamp. They were perfect copies of the mitten Gran had made.

'*Oh!*' said Will. He didn't realize he'd said it until it was out of his mouth.

Mr Fitchet's head snapped up. Will stumbled backwards into the murk as the huge factory door creaked open. Light fell in a triangle on to the grass, and the dark silhouette of Mr Fitchet stepped into the doorway.

'Just what do you think you're doing?'

7

Will heard a rustling in the leaves behind him. He turned to see moonlight glinting on a pair of purple glasses. It was the short lady from that Gang of Grannies who had come to the house! She was wearing what looked like a long knitted cloak, and she was walking towards Will. To Will's surprise, however, she didn't look at him at all, but strode towards the building with her head in the air, staring at the man in the doorway.

'I could ask you the same thing,' she said, her voice clear and steady. 'If I'm not very much mistaken, you have stolen property on these premises.'

She was right up next to Will now, and as she passed, she swept the cloak off her with one hand, and flung it aside. Before he knew what had happened, the cloak had flown right over Will's head and covered him entirely.

For a second Will panicked, pulling his breath in so quickly his throat closed. But it only lasted an instant, before the cloak surrounded him with a soft *shhhh*, and he was breathing again, quiet and sure.

'I don't know what you're talking about, madam,' Mr Fitchet said. 'I shall call the police if you don't leave immediately. You are trespassing!'

Will looked through the tiny holes in the knitting and saw Purple Glasses pull herself up so that she almost seemed tall. 'I will warn you once,' she said in her deep head-teacher's voice. 'Leave Gertie's family alone. If you harm them, if you steal from them, if you harass them in any way, believe me, we will know.'

Gertie? She was talking about his own family!

'Is that supposed to frighten me?' Mr Fitchet's oboe voice became harsh. 'I insist that you leave my property, madam.'

'You have been warned,' said Purple Glasses. She turned and walked into the darkness towards Will, and the factory door slammed behind her.

As she passed she put her arm around Will.

'Come with me,' she said softly.

As they reached the riverbank, four white-haired figures ran out from the trees, rushing towards Will and Purple Glasses. It was the Gang of Grannies.

'Are you all right, Jun-Yu?'

'Did he have Will?'

'What did he steal?'

Purple Glasses raised one hand in the air and waited until the talking died down. Then she swept aside the arm that was holding the cloak around Will. 'He's safe.'

The grannies let out a quartet of sighs.

'Is that an *Invisibility Cloak*?' asked Will. This was getting more and more exciting.

'No,' said Purple Glasses. 'Not even your gran could *quite* do that. It's more like an Un-noticing Cloak. I pulled the hood down when he came out, so that he'd notice me instead of you. Then he didn't even see it was in my hands when I flung it over you.'

'My *gran* made it? How does it work? Are you really part of her knitting club?'

'So many questions! But this is not the place, Will. I'm not sure that we're safe here.'

Four white-haired heads snapped around, surveying the car park like a herd of deer catching a scent. The stout one, Will saw, was gripping a giant knitting needle.

'We should get Will home,' said the little sparrow-lady with the bun.

Will let them follow as he pushed his bike back up the hill. They stopped at the end of the alley.

'Can you meet us tomorrow?' whispered

Purple Glasses. 'At the knitting shop in Wool-wick Lane? We'll be there all morning.'

'I'll try,' said Will.

'Good lad. We'll watch to make sure you're in safely. Lock the door behind you — and lock your window too.'

Will wasn't smiling as his head hit the pillow for the second time that night, but he managed a chuckle before he fell asleep. Dad was right. There had been more to Gran than he'd ever imagined.

8

Will supposed that The Knittery had always been there. He'd just never noticed it before. It certainly looked at home in Woolwick Lane, which was lined with crooked, pointy houses, each looking like one of Gran's teapots. The shop window looked like the inside of Gran's house: full of knitting. There were green-striped socks, hats with fox and rabbit ears, and fluffy, speckled mittens. A clothes line stretched along the top was hung with spotted oven mitts, and jumpers for dogs in several sizes.

Will stood across the street, pretending he was waiting for the pasty shop to open. The

Knittery didn't seem like a place a boy would ever go. Finally he took a deep breath and, looking up and down the cobblestones to make sure no one he knew was nearby, he shot across to the shop.

A cluster of bells tinkled as he opened the door, like a winter sleigh in the snow. Inside, sunlight stretched across a red brick floor. Wooden cubicles lined the walls, crammed with balls of wool. Will found himself staring at the wall ahead of him. He'd never realized how many different kinds of blue there were: Superman blue, and Smarties blue, and biro blue. Blue-jeans blue, and swimming-pool blue, and blue like a summer bedtime sky.

'Bandits! Bandits!'

Will jumped and whirled around. Next to an old stone fireplace was a wooden table with a till on it. Behind it, a teenage girl in a red-and-pink striped sweater-dress and black Doc Marten boots sat cross-legged on a stool. She had two buns on top of her head with knitting needles stuck through them, and she

was knitting something huge and purple.

'Three o'clock!' she shouted.

'What?' asked Will.

'If we were standing on a giant clock face, and I was in the middle of it,' said the girl, 'you would be at three o'clock.' She had a crooked smile, as if everything was half-funny.

'Oh,' said Will. He was very confused.

'I'm Holly. Dorcas's granddaughter.'

Somewhere above their heads Will heard a voice. He thought it said, 'Send the tiddler up!'

'They're waiting for you,' she said. She nodded towards a narrow stairway in the corner between the reds and the yellows. 'Up there.'

The staircase wound round, like a staircase in a castle. When he came to the top of it,

Will stepped into a room with a steeply sloping ceiling and huge timber beams. Around an oak table, with knitting in their hands, sat the Gang of Grannies.

'Will!' Purple Glasses jumped up and put an arm lightly around his shoulders, leading him to the table. 'Welcome to The Knittery!' She smelt of tangerines and fairy soap. 'Allow me to introduce Dorcas, Ivy, Matilda and Hortense. I am called Jun-Yu.'

'And you were . . . Gran's knitting club?' asked Will.

'Have a look, Will,' said Jun-Yu. She pulled a chair out for him and slid an old-fashioned photo album across the table, the kind with actual photos stuck on to the pages. Will opened it. In picture after picture, on page after page, he saw Gran with this Gang of Grannies. Here they were decorating Christmas trees; there they were cradling spring lambs; here they were singing Happy Birthday around a giant Victoria sponge. And everywhere they were knitting. Knitting in kitchens, gardens and tea shops; knitting at football and rugby matches. Knitting at morris dances. In one photo, labelled 'The Motomaids!' it even looked like they were knitting at a motorbike show, clacking away while girls in white minidresses rode motor-cycles through rings of fire.

'You see. We were your gran's team.'

'But,' said Will, 'how come we never knew you?'

'It's not terribly powerful, what we do, Will,' said Jun-Yu. 'But, as I think you under-stand by now, it is *magic*.'

'It's best to stay under the radar,' whispered Hortense, the tall one, waggling her eye-brows behind her round glasses. 'Sneaky beaky,' she said, tapping the side of her nose.

'And you all make . . . magic knitting?' asked Will.

Jun-Yu looked round at the others, who nodded at her.

'Yes,' she said. 'There are three ways. The first way is the pattern itself. Some patterns are simply powerful.'

'It's a bit like writing code,' said Hortense.

'And Gran knew how?' asked Will.

'Oh, your gran knew dozens of powerful patterns,' said Dorcas, the tiny little sparrow-lady.

'*Ve-e-e-ry* potent,' said Ivy, the one with the plaits.

'Top-hole stuff!' said Matilda, the one with the strong arms. She sounded like an Enid Blyton book.

'The second way,' said Jun-Yu, 'involves focusing on what you want the object to do as you knit it. Filling your mind and your heart with it.'

'Anyone who knits does a bit of this sort of magic knitting whenever they make things for someone they love,' said Dorcas, smiling.

'But a gifted practitioner with many years of practice can make it quite strong,' said Jun-Yu.

'That's why grans are best at it,' said Dorcas, her white bun jiggling as she nodded.

'*Your* gran was the bee's knees,' said Hortense.

'The kipper's knickers,' said Ivy.

'She thought big, Gertie did,' said Jun-Yu.

'Really?' asked Will. *Gran?* Gran was all about sticking plasters and gingerbread houses and tying shoes slowly enough to show how it was done. Gran was about fetching them from school when no one else could come, making knights out of tinfoil and games out of old sheep's fleece. Gran was all kinds of things . . . but not *big*.

'Before we met your gran,' said Jun-Yu, 'we each had little tricks that we used when we knitted for our families. One of us knew a way to make hats a bit warmer than they should be. Another could make blankets a little more comforting. One of us knew how to make soft toys that could put a baby to sleep. But your gran, she was in another league.'

'She could help people heal after surgery,' said Ivy.

'She could stop the nightmares of soldiers who came back from war,' said Hortense.

'She could make people calmer, kinder and wiser,' said Dorcas.

'She's the one who recruited us,' said Hortense, pushing her glasses further up her nose. 'She'd turn up wherever there was knitting. Cricket matches. Parish council meetings. The WI. She'd spot anyone who was gifted, and strike up a conversation.'

'Grandchildren. Currant jam. Dahlias,' said Dorcas.

'Size you up. Then rope you in,' said Matilda.

'And then – only when she was sure of you – she'd tell you about the third way.'

'The third way?' asked Will.

The grans all looked at each other again.

'The third way is Magic Wool,' said Jun-Yu.

If anyone had tried to tell Will that there was such a thing as magic wool a fortnight ago, he would have nodded politely and assumed that the person was mad as a box of frogs. But because it was *this* week, he said, 'Oh. Where does that come from?'

'We don't know,' said Dorcas softly.

They were quiet for a moment.

'And we've almost run out,' said Ivy.

'But Gran knew?' asked Will.

Jun-Yu nodded. 'Only one person in a knitting knot knows, you see – in order to keep the secret safe – and that was your gran.'

'A knitting knot?'

'That's what we call a knitting club,' Jun-Yu explained. 'Your gran called our knot together for a meeting just before she died. We think she was going to tell us more about the Magic Wool, because she knew she was ill. But then – well, there wasn't time in the end.'

'But what about Mr Fitchet?' said Will. 'He stole those mittens from my house – and Sophie's dog. He must have known that Gran could make magic.'

'He's up to some kind of jiggery-pokery, that's for sure,' said Hortense, shaking her head.

'He said he used to know Gran,' said Will. 'A long time ago.'

'I feel *sure* I remember his name,' said Dorcas, looking down at her knitting as if it might be written there. She was the most wrinkled of the grans, with the whitest hair. 'But I can't remember how.'

'What about your Memory Shawl?' said Ivy.

'Can't remember where I've put it!' said Dorcas.

'Well, whatever he's doing in that factory,' said Matilda, 'it's not cricket.'

'He was studying the patterns of the mittens,' said Will. 'And I think he copied them into his computer.'

'I do NOT like the sound of that,' said Ivy, shaking her head so fiercely her silver plaits swung out in an arc and smacked her on the nose.

'Let's not get in a flap, now,' said Jun-Yu. 'None of the patterns we've used – and none of the patterns Gertie ever used – will help the wearer do evil. And as far as we know, you can't make them in a factory, no matter how many old knitting mills you buy. It doesn't work like that. Each garment needs your full attention.'

'I'm sure it couldn't work without a talented pair of hands,' said Matilda firmly.

'I'm sure it couldn't work without love,' said Dorcas.

'And it would only be *really* powerful,' Hortense dropped her voice low, 'if he had *Magic Wool*.'

'He took little bits of wool out of the mittens he stole,' said Will. 'The sparkly bits.'

There was silence.

'Nobody panic,' said Jun-Yu. 'The wool will *not* let itself be used for anything bad. We *know* that.'

'Won't *let* itself?' asked Will.

'It will simply unravel.'

'It can also make you feel *really* sick,' said Ivy, with a sideways glance at Will.

'And it is extremely unlikely that he'll be able

63

to get hold of very much of it,' said Jun-Yu.

'Not that the blighter hasn't tried,' said Matilda.

'He's been haunting the Oxfam shop, where your gran's things ended up,' said Ivy to Will.

'But so have we,' said Hortense. 'The shop is sorting through it bit by bit, so we have to keep checking.'

'Aren't there any – oh, I don't know – knitting police?' asked Will.

Jun-Yu sighed. 'There is an organization called the Knitwork. Gertie was a member. And we know that the head of the Knitwork is called—' She stopped.

'The Knitwitch,' Ivy whispered.

'But we've never met her,' said Matilda.

'Or any of them,' said Dorcas.

'It's all don't-call-us-we'll-call-you,' said Hortense, waggling her eyebrows.

'Oh, I do wish they *would* call,' said Ivy. 'We were doing some good work with the Magic Wool, and we could keep on doing it, if only we could get hold of some more!'

'I'm sure in time they'll get word that we've lost the leader of our knitting knot,' said Jun-Yu with certainty, 'and they'll send someone down to sort us out.' She looked over the top of her purple glasses as if daring anyone to contradict her.

'*If* they think we're good enough without Gertie,' Ivy muttered.

'Why don't we just go and knock on his door, ask what he's playing at and take our stuff back?' asked Will. 'He was bang out of order stealing those mittens. I hardly even got to try them on!'

'I'm not sure that would be prudent,' said Jun-Yu.

'Seems a bit of a loose cannon, that one,' said Matilda.

'Don't trouble trouble if trouble doesn't trouble you,' added Dorcas.

'Safest to give him a wide berth for now, I think,' said Jun-Yu, with a brisk nod. 'I've given him a warning, and when the Knitwork arrives, they'll sort him out.'

Will hoped she was right.

'There's one other thing,' he said, trying to think how to ask, then deciding to come right out with it. 'Will you teach me to knit?'

All the grans smiled fit to burst.

'We thought you'd never ask,' said Ivy.

9

'Why are you wearing your dad's socks, Will?' asked Mum.

It was fete day in Knittington, and Mum, Will and Sophie were on their way to the abbey grounds.

'Because they're magic and they make me jump higher, and I want to show Ben!' said Will. He had to force himself not to bounce out into the road at the pelican crossing.

'Magic? Oh, yes, that'll be it!' Mum laughed.

The abbey grounds smelt of cut grass and roses and hot sausage rolls. Accordions were pumping and bells were jingling, and morris dancers with daisies on their hats bobbed and leapt in the middle of the grass. Along the edges of the grounds tables stood under marquees, some spread with lemonade, tea and cake, others covered with jumble and old books. In one corner a bouncy castle trembled, and in another people were throwing cricket balls at a stand full of mismatched old crockery.

Will scanned the grounds looking for Ben, who lived three doors down and had just come back from holiday the night before. He was itching to see if the two of them could wear one sock each and power-hop together.

'He's absolutely *lovely*!' Mrs de Rupertville was saying to Mum. '*Such* a gentleman! And he's been *so* kind about the fete.' A bored Sophie hung on to Mum's hand and leant backwards, swinging back and forth as Mrs de Rupertville continued: 'I said to him, I said, "Mr Fitchet, it is *so* refreshing to have someone in Knittington who knows how things should be done."'

Will's ears pricked up. Fitchet again.

'And I don't mind telling you he's been *very* generous with donations,' Mrs de Rupertville continued. 'Just wait until you see what he's done about prizes for the duck race!'

They followed the crowd towards the river. 'Even Mrs de Rupertville likes Mr Fitchet,' Mum muttered. 'Never mind that she's been trying to have that old mill torn down for a decade.'

'One. Pound. Per. Duck,' Sophie read, as they stood in the queue for ducks. 'Cash Prizz-es.'

'Prizes,' said Will. Sophie could never rest until every printed word she could see had been deciphered.

'What's that say on the balloon, Will?' On the bank of the river a giant hot air balloon rippled in the breeze.

'Fitchet & Ferret,' said Will, frowning.

'Right!' said Mum. 'I've got three tickets, for three ducks. Let's get to the river!'

The crowd pushed on to the riverbanks. It

smelt fresh and leafy and wet here, and under the noise of chatter was the bubbling rush of river on rock. Will spotted Mr Wood from the allotments standing on the bridge next to Bicycle Bob, and Miss Violet in the garden of the Fleece, near Ben and his parents. Will waved across at Ben.

Two men in waders and high-vis jackets stepped into the water with long poles, and the crowd began to count down. 'Ten – nine – eight – seven –'

The vicar took hold of the cord attached to the net of yellow plastic ducks that hung above the water from the branch of a willow.

'Three – two – one!'

The vicar tugged the cord, and the ducks spilt into the river. None of their ducks won anything – in fact, Mum's was third to last – but the race was still fun to watch.

'And now,' said Reverend Elaine, standing on the stone bridge after the ducks had all reached the finish line, 'the kind – and, I must say, very generous – sponsor of this year's duck race is here to give out the prizes. Allow me to introduce one of Knittington's own, back after many years' absence, with exciting plans to revitalize industry here: Mr Jasper Fitchet.'

Everyone applauded as Mr Fitchet stepped on to the bridge. He smiled his twinkly-eyed, pressed-tight grin, and raised his hand up in the air. 'Thank you, vicar, thank you,' he said, taking her hand in both of his and looking into her eyes. 'You're too kind. I only want to give back to Knittington some of what it gave to me. And that starts here, with this year's duck race winners.'

Besides the hefty cash prizes for the first three winners, everyone whose duck had finished in the first twenty places got to pick a parcel out of a huge sack.

'I wonder what's in the parcels?' asked Sophie.

'Probably something Mr Fitchet is making in his new factory,' said Mum.

'Look! Ben's dad won one!'

'And Bicycle Bob!'

'Nearly time for the piggy-back race,' said Mum. 'Did you two want to enter that?'

Of course they did. They'd been practising all week. Their speciality was the flying mount, where Sophie came at a run and jumped up on to Will's back. It gave them an extra push at the start.

'Ready . . .' called Reverend Elaine. 'Steady . . .'

Behind him, Will could hear Sophie taking her running start.

'GO!'

Whack! Sophie landed on his back and Will surged forward, shooting ahead of the crowd. He'd never gone so fast before. This was faster than they'd ever managed, even with the flying mount. They were practically airborne! What was going on?

'Woah!' said Ben, from Rafi's back.

'Blimey!' said Olive and Annie.

'Ugh!' said Will, falling to his knees. He smashed on to his stomach with Sophie on

top of him. He felt ill. Like flu ill. Like seasick ill. And his feet were on fire. He'd forgotten about the socks.

Sophie scrambled off his back and sat up in the grass, laughing, while Will ripped his shoes off and tore the socks from his feet. The sparkly heels were hanging in shreds. They had unravelled themselves.

'Are you all right, Will?' Mum was kneeling down in the grass beside them. 'Did you trip in those giant socks? Oh, I shouldn't have let you wear those!'

Will rolled the socks into a tight ball, and put his trainers back on without them. It had nothing to do with tripping, and he knew it. It was because he'd been about to cheat, and the Magic Wool wouldn't allow him to. *The wool will not let itself be used for anything bad,* Jun-Yu had said.

Mum was now fussing over Sophie, who had a grazed knee but was still laughing and saying, 'Let's do it again!' Meanwhile, the race was finishing, and Ben and Rafi came in third. Will, Mum and Sophie stayed to watch them choose packages from the big bag of prizes.

'Wotcha, Wills!' said Rafi, strolling over with the package under his arm. He had three older brothers and sometimes talked like them.

Will stuffed the socks deeper into his jacket pocket. Maybe he wouldn't tell Ben about them today. Rafi would never believe it.

'Bad luck, Will!' said Ben. 'You'd have finished before us for sure, with that start!'

'Nah,' said Will. 'You guys were great. What's in the packages?'

It was jumpers. Knitted hoodies with zigzag stripes the colour of acid drops that almost seemed to be moving. If you looked closely, there were tiny black flecks all over them. They felt horribly itchy.

'Creepy,' said Ben.

'Mental,' said Rafi.

'Fantastic!' said Mum. Will looked at her sideways. Was she just being polite? 'And what are those envelopes in the bottom of the package?'

They were announcements of the grand opening of Fitchet & Ferret, together with vouchers to spend on the day.

'Isn't that lovely?' said Mum absent-mindedly.

Strange, thought Will. It didn't look like her kind of thing. Ben and Rafi didn't look impressed either.

'Oh, well, Dad'll be happy,' said Ben. 'He loves his.'

They all looked across the grass to where Ben's dad was walking towards them. He was wearing a jumper with zigzag stripes of toothpaste green, mustard yellow and pale orange the colour of sick. As he came closer Will could see it was sprinkled all over with tiny black flecks.

'Hey! Aren't these great? I wish you had one — don't you wish you had one?' Ben's dad was talking much more quickly than usual. 'I mean, wow! This is exactly what I need and I didn't even know I needed it until I actually saw it and then it was mine so how lucky is that!'

Ben's forehead creased into puzzled squiggles. Rafi laughed, glancing around at the others. 'Wow, Mr Hobbs,' he said. 'Dude.'

Just then drums and fiddles started playing. Dad's band was playing for the scary morris dancers, the ones with the masks and black hats, and Sophie loved them. They all moved to the middle of the green to watch. While the sticks crashed and Sophie screamed, Will decided he was glad they hadn't won the piggyback race. He didn't want to touch anything made in Jasper Fitchet's factory.

10

'And look what happened to them!' said Will, holding Dad's socks up by their shredded golden heels. It was the day after the fete, and Will was upstairs at The Knittery. It had turned out that Mum took yoga with Matilda's daughter, and Dorcas had a grandson in Sophie's class, so Will was allowed to go and knit with the Gang of Grannies whenever he liked, as long as he wasn't a nuisance.

'Pep-In-Your-Step Socks!' said Dorcas, smiling her thousand-wrinkle smile. 'Good for tired, run-down people. Has your dad been ill?'

'He had pneumonia last year.'

'That'll be when Gertie made these, bet you a button,' said Dorcas.

'Can we re-use that Magic Wool?' asked Will. 'Could I make new socks?' Besides having ruined the fun, Will felt bad about destroying Dad's socks.

'There are several steps you need to pass through before you can use Magic Wool,' said Jun-Yu.

'What steps?' asked Will.

Just then Hortense ducked into the room through the open window, with binoculars hung round her neck. She had to fold her tall body nearly in half to get through.

'Well?' asked Matilda. Hortense had been on the roof of Jun-Yu's flat, at the back of The Knittery, spying on the factory. 'What's the little blighter up to?'

'Milk bottles!' said Hortense, her eyes as round as her glasses. 'Mr Fitchet is having milk delivered to him at the mill.'

'You don't say,' said Ivy, without looking up from her knitting. She had her feet up on the table, showing off flowered leggings. Ivy always wore something flowered. 'How dastardly!'

'What steps?' asked Will again.

'Well,' Jun-Yu said, nudging the purple glasses up her nose, 'first you need to have been knitting steadily for a year.'

Will rolled his eyes. 'A year?'

Jun-Yu nodded firmly.

'There's nothing done without trouble, dear boy,' said Dorcas, 'except letting the fire go out.'

'And then, old bean,' said Matilda, 'you need to learn Harkening Stitch.'

'What's Harkening Stitch?' asked Will.

'It's the most important stitch of all,' said Hortense.

'And the hardest,' said Ivy.

'But you need it for every powerful pattern,' said Dorcas.

'What does it do?' asked Will.

'It makes you heed your Best Self,' said Jun-Yu.

'Heed?' asked Will.

'Listen to,' said Ivy. 'It makes you follow your conscience.'

'We only teach it when we're sure the person has taken to knitting,' Jun-Yu went on, 'and only if we think they're persistent and reliable. Once the person masters it, they make a whole Harkening Jumper, and then we know we can trust them to be magical knitters.'

'Ha!' said Holly, who was coming up the stairs with a large tea tray. 'Or maybe they'll make you knit *three* Harkening Jumpers and then *still* say you're not ready!' *Thunk.* She put the tray down on top of the unravelled socks.

'Thank you, dear,' said Jun-Yu, sliding the tray off the socks. All the grans treated the things knitted by Gran as if they were sacred artefacts.

'Have you really made three Harkening Jumpers?' asked Will.

'Well. Two and a half,' said Holly.

'We just want to make sure you are solid in the basics,' said Jun-Yu. 'You can't be too cautious.'

'Can't you?' said Holly. She turned to Will. 'Your jumper looks like a Harkening one.' He'd worn it every day since he'd chosen it at Gran's.

'I've been itching for a look at that jumper, Will,' said Jun-Yu. 'I wonder if you'd mind . . .'

Will took the jumper off, while Jun-Yu pulled the lamp closer to the table. She held the jumper gently, as if it was a newborn baby, and laid it down in the glow of the lamp. 'Sure enough,' she said after a minute. 'Solid Harkening Stitch.'

'I can spot it at fifty metres by now,' said Holly, crossing her arms.

'It makes me feel happy when I wear it,' said Will.

'Being your Best Self always does,' said Dorcas.

'Have a look at this,' said Jun-Yu. 'Have you noticed this little bee embroidered on the inside of the wrist?'

Will nodded. It was about the size of a five-pence coin, and silky smooth. He had no idea why Gran had put it there. 'She never put it in anything else she made us. Sometimes our initials, but never a little picture like that.'

'How odd that it's got Magic Wool in it too,' said Hortense, pointing to the stripe with the gold running through it.

'Normally Harkening Jumpers don't,' Jun-Yu explained. 'Because people don't know about Magic Wool until they finish making theirs.'

'Is it . . . Gran's Harkening Jumper?' asked Will.

'Oh, no,' said Jun-Yu. 'No, this not a beginner's jumper. Your gran made this jumper for someone else.'

'I think I remember her working on that,' said Hortense. 'It was just before Easter.'

'So,' asked Will, 'a person can make a Harkening Jumper for someone else?'

'It's best when you make your own,' said Jun-Yu. 'But it might be nearly as effective if someone really skilled made one for you. And if they put Magic Wool in it.'

'Can I start one now?' Will asked.

'How about if we begin with something a bit simpler and see if you actually like knitting first,' said Dorcas, with a smile. Will remembered that he had kind of hated knitting when Gran had tried to teach him once. But that was before he knew what knitting could do.

'If you want to do really powerful knitting you need to quiet your mind,' said Ivy, putting her knitting down and looking at Will with her shimmery eyes. She was the only one of the grans who wore make-up, and it usually sparkled. 'It's not so important now, but it will be later. So close your eyes.'

Will felt really silly, but he closed his eyes.

'Now put all your other thoughts down until there is nothing in your head except the sounds around you.'

Will listened. He heard pigeons chuckling on the roof, and bees buzzing outside the window.

'There,' said Ivy. 'Now open your eyes.'

'It starts like this,' said Dorcas, holding up two needles that she'd been fiddling with in her tiny wrinkled hands. 'Around, under, through, off.' She handed the needles to Will. 'Around, under, through, off.'

'Around – under – through – '

'Would you like to hear the rhyme?' asked Dorcas. 'It's a bit babyish for a boy your age, but it might help all the same. It goes:

'In through the rabbit hole,
Round the big tree,
Up comes the rabbit,
And off goes she!'

'I know that rhyme,' said Will. 'We used to sing it with Gran. And there were other verses too.

'Under the fence,
Grab that sheep,
Out of the fence,
And off we leap!'

'Why, that's the rhyme for purling!' said Dorcas. 'Knit and purl are the two beginning stitches in knitting.'

'There were two more verses,' said Will.

'Gather from the hedges,
Golden in the dawn,
Wash it in the river,
Spread it on the lawn.'

'Card it with a carding comb,
Careful as you can,
Spin it with a spindle,
And give it to your gran.'

All of the grans put their knitting down. The church clock chimed in the silence.

'Well, cover me in feathers and call me a dodo bird,' said Ivy.

'Doesn't that sound like it could be . . .' said Jun-Yu.

'. . . a description of basic Harkening Stitch,' said Hortense.

'Your gran was coaching you before you

even knew there was such a thing as magic knitting!' said Dorcas.

'See!' said Will. 'She *wanted* me to make a Harkening Jumper!'

'No one said differently, child,' said Dorcas. 'All things in the fullness of time, that's all. It doesn't do to rush a Harkening Jumper.'

'Haste makes waste,' said Jun-Yu.

'Rome wasn't built in a day,' said Matilda.

'Adopt the pace of nature,' said Ivy. 'Her secret is patience.'

'The two most powerful warriors are patience and time,' said Hortense.

Holly snorted and put the tray under her arm. The knitting needles in her buns trembled as she stomped down the stairs. '*Someday* is not a day of the week!' she called over her shoulder.

11

For the next two weeks the weather was rainy, and Ben went on holiday again, so Will went to The Knittery nearly every day. During that time, he made a cape for his Iron Man, a scarf for Mum's birthday, and a soft green hat for himself (well, very nearly).

Will was so busy learning to knit, he didn't notice that strange things were happening around town. He wasn't the least bit interested when Mum said that only two people had showed up for bell-ringing practice. He barely heard Sophie pointing out that Miss Violet hadn't filled her bird feeders for three days. Even when he and Dad saw Bicycle Bob getting off the bus with two plastic shopping bags, it only seemed a little funny.

'Bob! What are you doing on a bus?' laughed Dad. 'I think that's the first time I've ever seen you in a combustion-fired vehicle.'

Bob looked startled. He held the bags up.

'My jumper's coming apart,' he said. He was sweating. 'I had to look for another one. I have to find one like it, *just* like it,' he said. He turned away, and walked off without saying anything at all about global warming.

'Quiet today,' said Mum, when she and Will went down to the allotments to harvest the runner beans. 'Has everyone gone on holiday?'

'Mr Wood doesn't go on holiday,' said Will, looking at the empty bench in the allotment next to theirs. 'Now that he's retired, he gardens every day, and it's like he's on holiday all year round.'

Mum laughed. 'Yes, he does say that, doesn't he?'

'Only every time we come,' said Will.

There was even trouble at Dad's museum, because none of the volunteers were turning up, so there was a pile of tasks that needed doing for the Summer Open Day. 'I guess that's one good thing to come out of our cancelled holiday,' said Dad. 'We never would have managed all of this if I'd been away.'

But things only started to seem seriously strange when Will stopped at Ben's house to welcome him home from his holiday.

'No cake?' asked Will. The Knittington Bake-Off was coming up, and Ben's dad loved baking. He usually went crazy for it.

'No,' said Ben. There was a package of pink wafers on the kitchen table. Ben picked it up and turned it over slowly, as if he'd never seen biscuits in a package before.

'Remember last year?' asked Will.

Ben laughed. 'That was epic!' There'd been three practice cakes in a row.

'What's he making this year?'

'He's not entering,' said Ben, still staring

at the pink wafers. 'Said he couldn't be bothered.'

'Oh,' said Will. He found himself staring at the pink wafers too. He wished he hadn't asked.

Will went home by the pavement instead of the back garden, and heard a rustle of paper as he opened the front door. Someone had pushed a bunch of flyers through the letter box. Will stepped back out on to the path and scooped the papers up from the hall floor. (His magic jumper was making him very helpful.) He might as well drop them in the recycling as long as he was here at the front. He had just lifted the lid to the recycling bin when he glanced down at the flyers in his hand.

Fitchet & Ferret, said the flyer on top. *Where 1% wool makes all the difference. Come to our Grand Opening!*

Will put the bin lid down. He slid the top flyer aside to see the next one.

Are you looking for a special jumper? it

said. *One that makes you feel alive? Come to the grand opening of Fitchet & Ferret. We'll make all your dreams come true.*

The third one just said, *Fitchet & Ferret. You'll never get enough.*

Suddenly, in spite of his magic jumper, Will shivered.

12

That evening Holly came to babysit for them.

'Right!' she said as the front door closed behind Mum and Dad. She thumped her purple rucksack down on the kitchen table and pulled a pair of binoculars out of it. 'Can we get out on to your roof?' she asked.

Will blinked.

'Not easily,' he said. 'But Sophie and I both have our rooms on the top floor, and you can see quite a lot from up there.'

'I want a view of the factory.'

Sophie's room looked down on the tiny front gardens, where there were bicycles and wheelie bins and ivy, and every house looked the same. But Will's room looked out over the back gardens, where everything was different. From up here you could see trampolines and gazebos and sheds; a vegetable patch, a bee hive, and a chicken coop; a tent, a canoe and a cider press. You could see the striped flowers in Arthur and Rosie's garden, Mr Wade's miniature village with a train going round the edge, and Olive and Annie's hedgehog hospital. Right now, the Pingles were shooting longbows, the Riders were photographing their fossil collection, and down at the end, the morris dancers were rehearsing.

'Ah,' said Holly, focusing. 'Better view here. I live at Gran's farm, just on the edge of town, and I can't see anything but the abbey steeple from our roof. You can see the mills here, between the trees.'

'There's a good view from the roof of The Knittery too,' said Will. 'Hortense can see into some of the factory windows.'

'I know,' said Holly. 'But she doesn't look often enough.'

'Can we play a game?' asked Sophie.

Holly put the glasses down. 'How about you show me a game and I'll show you one?'

'Cronk says we should play Fluff-in-the-Faddle.'

Will looked across the passage into Sophie's room. The cat was sitting like a sphinx on Sophie's bed, his yellow eyes closed, and his strong legs tucked under him. Cronk had no tail, because he was a sort of cat that doesn't, but he was nearly always lying down, so it didn't show.

'It looks to me like Cronk's asleep,' said Will. 'In fact, he's pretty much

always asleep, as far as I can tell.'

'I'm sure Cronk knows what he's talking about,' said Holly. 'You know, we used to play Fluff-in-the-Faddle with my gran too.'

'Really?' said Will. He'd thought *their* gran had invented it.

The faddles were bags full of fluffy sheep's wool that Gran had let them play with because it wasn't a kind of wool that was good for spinning. Holly spread it on to the grass and the branches in the back garden, just like Gran used to do. Then Sophie and Will raced to see who could fill their bag first, and because Will was wearing his magic jumper, he let Sophie win.

'Now,' said Holly. 'Want to try my skipping rope?' She pulled a length of thin rope out of her bag.

Will pulled a face at first, but then he looked more closely. 'Did you *knit* a skipping rope?'

'Sort of crocheted,' she said. 'Yes, and it's a Holly Original. My own invention.'

'Can you *do* that?' asked Will. 'I mean, just

invent your own pattern?'

'Do you mean am I capable or am I allowed? Yes, not really, though I didn't actually ask.'

'Let's skip!' said Sophie.

They went out to the road in front of the terrace and Holly handed them each an end.

'Really?' said Will. He didn't want to be seen playing with a skipping rope in front of the whole street.

'I guarantee you, you are going to be the coolest kid in a half-mile radius in less than ten minutes,' she said.

She showed them how to turn the rope in big sweeping circles, and then she jumped into the middle. *Wwsh-skat, wwsh-skat*, went the rope. *Bounce-jump, bounce-jump*, went Holly, spinning in a circle as she skipped, looking all around the neighbourhood.

'Keep it up.' *Wwsh-skat.* 'Shouldn't be long now.' *Bounce-jump.*

'Hey! Can we play?' It was Isabelle and Robyn.

'Sure!' said Holly. 'Jump on in!'

'Can we have a turn?' It was Olive and Annie.

'Geronimo!' Holly jumped out of the way as Rafi and his brothers leapt through the rope. Sophie squealed with laughter.

Suddenly it seemed like the funnest thing in the world. More and more children were running into the street. 'Can we play?' Holly made everyone queue, beaming with smugness and directing the crowd with a nod of

her head while she swung the rope round. It was like a fun magnet, and the longer it went on, the funner it got. Rafi and his brothers started doing breakdance moves while they jumped, and instantly everyone was trying it. Ruby started doing cartwheels through the ropes and soon even Will was doing them.

Eventually mums and dads came out of front doors, looking for the younger ones. Holly had to drop the skipping rope and wind it up before they would go away.

'Does that have Magic Wool in it?' asked Will when they got back inside.

'Just a skrinsh,' said Holly, holding up two fingers pinched close together. 'I made it when I started at the big school and I was afraid no one would want to play with me.'

'Did you *steal* it?' asked Will.

'No!' said Holly in a voice like a screech owl. 'I'd been helping my gran with a big charity knit, and she said I could have some wool from her cupboard as a reward – anything I wanted. I could *feel* that the sparkly wool was special, so I took some.'

'Didn't any of them notice?'

'Oh they flipped when they clocked it! Especially your gran. That's why I had to make another Harkening Jumper, and then another. They're all afraid of inventing new patterns. It's even worse now that Gertie's gone. They won't make anything she didn't teach them. And she didn't teach them half of what she knew.'

'Stories!' said Sophie.

'As soon as you've brushed your teeth!' said Holly, following Sophie up the stairs. 'Something spooked your gran, I think,' she said to Will over her shoulder. 'Something made her scared to break the rules, or to tell anybody anything.'

Will brushed his teeth then went into Sophie's room and sat on the floor. 'So then the dragon came up behind Princess Holly,' Sophie was saying. 'It opened its hot, burning, flaming teeth, and it was about to eat her! Your turn.'

'But the princess had Seven-League Boots on,' said Holly. 'And so she just took one step and she was seven leagues away!'

'How far is seven leagues?' asked Sophie.

'Thirty-five kilometres,' said Holly. 'So the dragon couldn't catch her no matter how fast he was flying, because she'd just take a few steps in her magic boots and she'd be all the way in Helsinki! The End!'

They left the light on in the hallway for Sophie and tiptoed back to Will's window for a last look at the factory.

'I can see him,' said Holly. 'He's on the roof! Oh, ick! He's got binoculars too. I think he's looking at The Knittery!' She handed Will the glasses and shivered. 'Ugh, ugh, ugh! That's so creepy!'

Will took the glasses and pointed them down the hill. Sure enough, there was Jasper Fitchet standing on the roof of the old Wool-man Mill, with binoculars hooked over his small sharp nose.

'He is up to something seriously wonky!' said Holly. 'Whatever the grans say, we should be doing something about it.'

Will thought so too. But he didn't know what. And he didn't know what it would take to get the grans on side.

13

'Can I go to The Knittery?' asked Will when he came down for breakfast the next morning. The kitchen table was covered with papers, and Mum had her glasses on. She was biting both her lips, so her mouth looked like a thin crack. 'Are those Gran's things?' asked Will, seeing the flowery address book.

'Yes,' said Mum. 'I'm trying to finish up all of Gran's paperwork.'

'Can I help?' asked Will.

Mum smiled and pulled Will close, kissing the side of his head. 'Actually, there *is* something you could do,' she said. She pushed

Gran's laptop computer across the table. 'See if you can get into Gran's email. I can't work out the password, but you're so clever with these things.' She went to check on Sophie.

Will opened the computer and logged in as Gran. The password was just Will and Sophie's names. Easy-peasy. It felt funny going into someone else's computer, but if it was to help Mum and Dad, it must be OK.

Hmm. Would it also be OK if it helped the grans? If it helped all of them? Maybe there would be something here that might explain what was going on . . .

He looked at Gran's search history first. There were links to websites about knitting and the Isle of Man. He looked through some of them. Then he opened a folder called 'Photos'. They were mostly of Will and Sophie, but there was one of Gran herself. She was standing in a village of small white cottages, next to the craziest sheep Will had ever seen. It had four horns: two that curled down and two that stuck up. Now he thought about it, it looked an awful lot like his knitted pocket-sheep.

He clicked back on to one of the Isle of Man websites. There were pictures of the same kind of sheep. Manx Loaghtan sheep, they were called. Manx meant 'from the Isle of Man', Will remembered. Cronk was a Manx cat.

Gran's email inbox had only a handful of messages. The parish newsletter; something from the Woodlands Trust; an alert about a sale at a craft shop. And then there was one from NO REPLY, that was called URGENT. He clicked.

To all members of the Knitwork: A Rogue Knitter is at large in Great Britain. This Rogue is known to have offered magic knitwear for sale to athletes wishing to cheat in competitions, and to students seeking an unfair advantage in exams. He appears intent on innovation, in violation of all codes on the ethical use of Magic Wool. He is especially skilled in computerized knitting. If members spot anything suspicious, please contact the Knitwork by the usual means as soon as possible.

Reminder: The Golding Dawn begins at 5:33 a.m. on 25th August. Fleece pick-up as scheduled. Mum's the word when it comes to your herd.

Will stared. He started reading the note over again but before he'd got halfway through, it vanished from the screen. It was like an invisible hand had deleted it.

Will swallowed. With sweating hands he grabbed a notepad from the pile of papers and, scrawling as quickly as he could, wrote down everything he could remember of the message, especially the date and time of 'The Golding Dawn', whatever that was.

He stopped writing. All at once, he remembered being out with Gran in a moonlit meadow in the middle of a summer's night. It was so long ago that she was carrying him. She gave him fruit pastilles and they watched the dawn. It was some kind of game. She asked him to look hard at the sheep, to see if he could see any of them sparkling *gold*. He didn't know where or when it had been. And sadly, he was pretty sure he hadn't seen any sheep turning gold.

'Did you get in?' asked Mum, coming back into the kitchen.

'Er – yes,' said Will.

'Brilliant!' She came and stood behind Will's chair. 'Anything important?' Will typed the password in and got the screen to open up again. But the email had definitely disappeared.

'Just stuff about knitting,' said Will. But knitting, he now knew, could be *very* important.

'Thank you, darling,' said Mum, as Will got up from the chair. 'That's a big help.'

It has to be him, Will thought, swallowing a bite of boiled egg without tasting it. *Jasper Fitchet is the Rogue Knitter.*

14

Will was at The Knittery as soon as it opened, but he'd only taken one step into the shop before Jun-Yu called out, 'Stop!'

The floor looked like one of Sophie's giant finger paintings, but instead of swirls of paint, it was made with swirls of coloured yarn. The Knittery had been ransacked. Will felt like he was seeing someone's insides.

'Oh, my giddy aunt!' said Dorcas, who had come in behind him.

'Crikey!' said Matilda, who came in next. 'This is a rum do, isn't it?'

'Flaming Nora!' said Ivy. 'It looks like someone set an animal loose in here!'

'Sabotage!' said Hortense. 'That twoccer's after our Magic Wool!'

'Should we ring the Old Bill?' asked Matilda.

'If you mean the police, they've been and gone,' said Jun-Yu. 'They think I'm batty, of course. I told them it was ferrets.'

'Well, let's not just stand here,' said Matilda, looking from the floor to the empty cubicles on the walls.

'Many hands make light work,' said Dorcas.

'Sound action sta-tions!' called Hortense. 'We shall beat to quar-ters!'

'Last one done's an old brown mule!' said Ivy.

They spent the next hour sorting the wool back into its colour-coded niches. Three skeins of sparkly pink yarn were missing, but it wasn't Magic Wool. 'It's the stuff people use for making Anna and Elsa mittens,' Ivy snorted. Four skeins of Soay sheep wool from Scotland were also gone, 'which is closer to the mark, and hurts in the purse,' said Dorcas.

'But they didn't find the real stash!' said Hortense.

'Well, of course they didn't!' said Jun-Yu.

The last few bits of Magic Wool owned by the Gang of Grans were wrapped in lavender-scented tea towels, which were packed in a picnic hamper, which was locked in a cedar chest, which was shut in the loft.

'Still, I'm all joppity-joppity, and that's the truth,' said Dorcas.

'It's worse than you think,' said Will. He told them everything he could remember from the email.

'Oh. My. Word,' said Dorcas.

'Tea,' said Jun-Yu. 'Nice hot tea, all round.' She went into the kitchen.

'And you say it finished with a date in August?' asked Ivy.

'And the time of sunrise,' said Will. 'I think that's what the Golding Dawn is. I think the fleece turns gold then. And I found all sorts of links to websites for the Isle of Man. We were going to go on holiday with Gran there this year.'

'Were you, now?' said Dorcas.

'And you'd have been there on this date?' asked Ivy.

'Yes,' said Will. 'Next week.'

'We always thought it was Scotland,' said Hortense.

'She brought us back that cracking shortbread,' said Matilda.

'Not to mention the Drambuie!' said Ivy.

'But not last time, remember? Was it three years ago? When she got Cronk,' said Matilda.

'That's right. She brought us kippers,' said Ivy.

'And cake. Bonnag, was it called?' asked Matilda

'Bonnag, yes, that was it,' said Dorcas. 'I meant to look up a recipe, but I forgot.'

Hortense pulled out a phone, quickly tapping and swiping. 'Look!' she said, turning the screen around for the rest to see. 'Bonnag is a cake from the Isle of Man!'

'Well, pour me in a greased tin and bake me for an hour!' said Ivy.

Rattling teacups clattered in the silence as Jun-Yu came in with a tea tray. 'What did I miss?'

'Bonnag,' said Ivy.

'Well, I have scones,' said Jun-Yu, looking annoyed.

'It comes from the Isle of Man,' said Dorcas.

'Where Cronk came from,' said Matilda.

'Where Gertie was going on holiday with Will and Sophie next week,' said Hortense.

Jun-Yu put the tray down. 'Oh, my,' she said. 'I see.' Then she straightened up and put her hands on her hips. 'Right,' she said. 'So, do we go?'

'To the Isle of Man? Oh, happy day!' said Ivy, pulling on her plaits as if to keep herself from floating away.

'It was Gertie's research,' said Hortense. 'We have to continue the work.'

'And if we're right, it might be our one chance to get Magic Wool for a whole year,' said Matilda.

'But we have no idea where or how to gather this fleece,' said Jun-Yu, shaking her head. She took her hands off her hips and sat down. 'The Knitwork can't expect us to act when they have all the information and we have none. Surely they'll have someone else on it.'

'But we want to continue as a knitting knot,' said Hortense. 'We want to be part of the Knitwork. Let's show them what we can do.'

'Let's go!' said Will. 'Let's try! Gran would want us to!'

'Well, we couldn't take you anyway, Will,' said Jun-Yu. 'Your parents would never give us permission. And it might be dangerous.'

'It's a moot point,' said Ivy, holding up her phone. 'Booked, booked, booked. This week is the TT.'

'You mean that crazy thing where they

race round the island on motorbikes?' said Jun-Yu. 'I thought that was in June.'

'It is,' said Ivy. 'But this week is the *classic* TT. Vintage motorbikes from all around the world will be gathering to race. The ferry to the island will have been booked since Christmas.' She sighed.

'She used to ride,' Hortense whispered to Will, who tried not to look surprised.

'So we can't get there anyway,' said Jun-Yu.

They sat still. The pigeons on the roof made sounds like sighs.

'But we have to do *something*,' said Will. 'He's also watching *us*.' He told them about seeing Fitchet on the roof. 'Jasper Fitchet's after Magic Wool, and he'll do anything to get it.'

'Hmm,' said Hortense. 'But if he's really watching us, the last thing we should do is lead him to the magic sheep.'

'Precisely,' said Jun-Yu. 'Let's not lose our heads, now. Keep calm and knit on.'

'But—' said Will.

Jun-Yu put a hand on his shoulder and said gently, 'As long as he doesn't know where to get Magic Wool, everything will be fine.'

15

Will knew there was something wrong as soon as he woke up the next morning. Something missing. Something Not Right. He shook his clothes on, and stepped out into the upstairs hallway.

The Not-Right thing was the sound. He thought at first it was the cricket on the radio, but it wasn't. It was the telly. Will went downstairs, past the open door to Dad's empty study, and into the living room. Dad was sitting in his pyjamas on the sofa eating a doughnut. He wasn't even wearing his glasses.

'Dad! You're watching the shopping channel!' said Will. Dad only ever watched programmes about castles or the plague.

Dad shrugged. 'Well, why not?'

'But you don't *like* those things,' said Will.

'Don't I?' asked Dad, and he laughed. It didn't sound like his laugh. 'Well, I seem to like it this morning!' He turned back to the TV screen. It was then that Will noticed Dad was wearing a jumper over his pyjamas. It was pale yellow-green, with little black flecks in it, and stripes the colour of wet concrete.

'Dad, where did you get that horrible jumper?'

'Quiet, Will,' said Dad, without even looking at him. 'I'm watching something important.'

Will backed out of the living room. He found Sophie in the kitchen eating a giant bowl of Cookie Puffs.

'Dad let you eat those?' The Cookie Puffs had been in the back of the cupboard since Uncle Robert had visited.

'Yes!' said Sophie, her eyes wide. 'He just poured them out for me and went to watch telly.'

That was the missing thing, Will realized suddenly. The smell of bacon. Usually Dad and Sophie made a cooked breakfast on Saturday mornings, while Mum had a lie-in — at least until Mr Rover started playing his bagpipes. Come to think of it, it was awfully quiet. He went to the back door. There was no sound from Mr Rover's. And the Pingles weren't trying out their massive catapult. Even Arthur and Rosie's striped garden was deserted.

Will poured himself a bowl of the Cookie Puffs and ate it slowly. He'd wanted some for months. But they weren't as good as he'd thought they'd be.

Things didn't get any less weird when Mum came down. She made coffee instead of tea, and hardly seemed to notice Will and Sophie. 'We had Cookie Puffs for breakfast,' Will announced, staring as Mum stirred three spoonfuls of sugar into her mug.

'Brilliant!' said Mum, smiling like someone on a toothpaste advert. 'That sounds yummy!' There was something wrong with her face.

'Do you . . . do you want some?' asked Will, looking hard at Mum. It was her eyebrows, he realized. They'd been painted on and they looked like long, fat squiggly slugs.

'Not hungry!' said Mum, smiling that weird smile again as she took a long drink from the giant mug.

'Mum,' said Will, 'where did you get that jumper?' It was Disney-princess pink, with tiny black flecks, and sparkly fake diamonds stuck all over.

'This?' said Mum, looking down at herself. 'It came in the post yesterday – from Fitchet & Ferret. Pretty, isn't it?'

Will didn't think so at all, but he didn't say it. It didn't look like Mum.

'But maybe you won't want to wear it to story hour,' said Will, trying to think fast. 'I mean, it's a bit fancy for the library.'

'Oh, I don't want to go to *story hour*

today!' said Mum. 'I want to go shopping for more clothes!' She bent down and ruffled Sophie's hair. 'How about that, cupcake?'

'You mean, like, go to the charity shops?' asked Will. That was where Mum usually went for clothes. She loved saying, 'charity shop!' whenever anyone told her she looked nice.

'Nah!' said Mum. 'Sophie and I want new, *fashionable* things, don't we?'

Sophie looked from the Cookie Puffs box to her empty cereal bowl, and back up at Mum. 'Could we get a dog?' she asked.

'How about a new jumper instead?' said Mum. 'You don't have to come if you don't want to, Wills,' she continued. (*Wills?*) 'You'll probably be bored. Why don't you go and play some games on Dad's computer while we're out?'

'*What?*' asked Will. He was only allowed half an hour of screen time a day, measured with an old oven timer that always went off just as things were getting interesting. But there was no way Will could let Mum go out on her own while she was acting like this. 'No, I want to come with you,' he said.

He paused for just a second on their way out, to look into the living room at Dad. Should he stay behind? What if the ferrets came back while they were gone and took Gran's cushions? Dad probably wouldn't even notice.

But then Mum swept past him with Sophie's hand clasped in hers. 'We're going to get new jump-ers! We're going to get new jump-ers!' she sang.

Will rushed out after them.

'*F*resh strawberries! Two pound a punnet! *Fresh* strawberries!'

Mum wouldn't look at any of the things she usually bought as they crossed the marketplace. She didn't even smell the basil.

'*Local* tomatoes! Two pound a bag! *Local* tomatoes!'

'What about the egg lady?' said Will, running to keep up. 'And don't you want flowers from the Hippy Farm? Blackberries? We could make crumble!'

'Nah!' said Mum. 'All that cream will make me fat! Besides, who wants to cook?'

'I do!' said Will. Suddenly he'd have given

anything to be chopping up apples in the kitchen.

'Such a waste of time making anything when you can just buy it!' said Mum. 'I'll buy you some sweets if you want pudding.'

Sophie stumbled as Mum pulled her across the street. Will trotted after them. Down the hill they went, Mum stopping in front of every shop window, and Sophie bumping into her legs each time. They were headed towards the stone bridge, which was draped with a huge sign saying: GRAND OPENING! FITCHET & FERRET! THIS WAY! The arrows were pointing towards Jasper Fitchet's factory.

'Oh, this is so exciting!' said Mum. 'A proper new shop down here in the old mills!' She gave Sophie an extra-strong yank as she strode up the bridge.

Will's heart was beating like a pile driver. He had to stop them.

The overgrown lot around the old Woolman Mill had been cleared, re-paved and lined with tubs of fake flowers. The wide wooden doors that led from the car park to the shop level were flung wide and hung with bunting. GRAND OPENING! said the sign over the doors. DELICIOUS DRESSES! FANTABULOUS FROCKS! TERRIFIC TIES! SENSATIONAL SWEATERS!

'Mum, I don't think we should go in there!' Will looked around wildly, hoping to catch sight of anyone who could help him. All he could see were people walking down to the new boutique from both sides of the river. Everyone wanted to shop.

'Don't be silly, darling!' said Mum, pulling Sophie into the building and leaving Will to follow.

The shop couldn't have looked more different from the basement below it. Instead of rough stone, there was a gleaming parquet floor. In place of the spider-shaped machines with their splayed steel legs, there were elegant sofas and vases full of sweet-smelling lilies. Headless mannequins, each wearing a knitted jumper or dress, hung from the ceiling, floating silently above the floor like phantoms. And instead of the rumble of knitting machines, there was the din of people buying things.

'Ooh, that's gorgeous!'

'Can I get some service here?'

'I'll take all three of them!'

A slender young woman with eyelashes like centipedes' legs smiled with candy-pink lips as Mum and Sophie walked in. 'Welcome to Fitchet & Ferret!' she said.

Mum let go of Sophie's hand and rushed towards a minidress all the colours of a mouldy orange, decorated with fake rubies. 'Oh. That is just *adorbs*!' she said.

'Everything is marked down to a hundred pounds today!' said another slender woman, who had nails like lobster claws.

Mum began running from one dress to another. 'I want to try on that one! And that one! And that one!'

'Mum! No!' said Will, following behind and pulling on her elbow. He tried to think of what Mum would say about these dresses when she was her normal self. 'I mean, do you think that's a natural fibre? I'm not sure you could recycle it.'

'Shall I bring these to a dressing room for you, madam?'

'Thank you!' said Mum.

Will wanted to rush into the dressing room behind Mum, and yank dresses out of her arms. But the slender young woman drew the velvet curtain closed as Mum went in.

Suddenly Will looked around him. 'Mum! Where's Sophie?' He looked under the curtain. All he could see were Mum's plimsolls and her big jute shopping bag on the floor.

'Oh, she's somewhere,' said Mum from behind the curtain. 'Don't worry! She's a big girl.'

'Sophie!' Will rushed through the hanging mannequins. 'Where's my little sister?'

The shop was fuller than ever. As he ran around the racks, Will was jostled, shoved, and hit in the face with an elbow. He'd never seen grown-ups act so rudely.

'That's mine!'

'I'll take that!'

Will froze. It was Bicycle Bob, wearing the jumper he'd won at the duck race. It was hanging in shreds, the sleeves dangling with loose strings. He was clutching at one sleeve of a new jumper and tugging. Pulling at the other sleeve was Ben's dad, in the jumper *he'd* won on fete day, which now looked like a ragged net.

'You don't understand,' said Bicycle Bob. 'I'm cold – I'm so cold.'

'But I *need* this jumper,' said Ben's dad. His eyes were round and he was sweating. 'Please, please.' He pulled the jumper towards him. Ben's dad pulled it back, clutching it to his chest.

Will couldn't stop to see what would happen. He ran to the dressing room. 'Mum, I can't find Sophie!'

'Who?' asked Mum.

'Sophie. *Our* Sophie! My sister!'

Will looked out of the door of the shop to the car park. Suddenly he felt very, very angry.

Jasper Fitchet was there. He had a ferret on a leash. Stepping up close to it, her hand outstretched, was—

'Sophie!' Will hurtled out on to the tarmac. 'Sophie! What are you doing?'

'I want to meet the ferret!' said Sophie.

'Your sister and I were just having a little chat about your summer holidays,' said Mr Fitchet. 'Only it was too noisy inside for my pet. What a shame it is that you aren't able to go to the Isle of Man with your granny. You'd be there right now, wouldn't you?'

Will ran to Sophie, and whirled her up in his arms. 'Stay away from my family!' he said to Fitchet.

'What on earth do you mean, dear boy?' said Fitchet calmly. The ferret was running back and forth around his neck and shoulders. 'There's no need for raised voices!'

'Yes, there is!' said Will. 'Just because

everyone else thinks you're Father Christmas doesn't mean I do. I *see* you, Jasper Fitchet!'

'Well, I did say you were a clever one.'

Will ran back through the open door of the shop with Sophie's arms and legs wrapped round him. This time he didn't stop outside the curtains, but went right into the dressing room, dumping Sophie on the stool next to the mirror. 'Stay right there, Sophie!' he said desperately.

Mum was standing

in her T-shirt, with a sparkly jumper in each hand. She blinked at Will and Sophie.

'Mum! Sophie just walked right out of the shop and into the car park with Mr Fitchet!'

Mum laughed that weird laugh again, but her forehead had sprouted a wrinkle. 'I'm sure it's all right, darling. She just— She just—'

'Mum. We have to get out of here. Now!' Will picked up Mum's shopping bag from the floor of the dressing room and was about to thrust it into her hand when he spotted something at the bottom of it. It was the patchwork cardigan Gran had made for Mum. Will whipped it out of the bag.

'Put this on,' he said, and he pressed it against her. Dropping the bag to the floor he grabbed both of her hands, forcing her to hold the cardigan.

'But—' Mum looked dazed.

Quickly Will gathered up all the sickly sparkly dresses in his arms and threw them out of the dressing room in a heap.

'Will, that's rude!' said Sophie.

'Well— But—' Mum was still dazed, but she was putting her arms into the cardigan sleeves. As she buttoned the front, she blinked down at Sophie and then at Will, her eyes finally looking into his.

'Did you say that your sister—?' She looked back at Sophie. 'Are you all right?' Swiftly she knelt down and lifted Sophie off the stool. Will grabbed the shopping bag with one hand, and Mum's sleeve with the other, tugging Mum along.

'Let's get out of here!' said Will, and this time Mum followed. 'Sorry about the mess!' she called on their way out. It sounded like her real voice now.

Jasper Fitchet was now back in the shop, with no sign of the ferret. He stepped in front of them and bowed.

'Well, hello, Mrs Shepherd,' he began. 'How very lovely to—'

'Don't listen to him!' shouted Will, pulling at Mum's arm. But Mum had become Mum again and she needed no pulling.

'I beg your pardon,' she said firmly, clutching Sophie closely to her as she stepped around the man. 'It's just that we're in a hurry, Mr Fitchet.'

'What a horrible shop that was,' she said as they came to the market stalls. 'I can't think why we went in there. The clothing was repulsive. Are you all right, Will?'

'Fine!' said Will, nodding hard. He was now.

Mum let Will hold the shopping bag and get the money out for the egg lady and the blackberry man and the hippy flower people. She didn't let go of Sophie the whole way home.

The telly was still on when they got back, and Dad was asleep on the sofa.

'He's been working too hard,' Mum said when she went in to check on him. He woke when she turned off the telly. 'John, where did you get that strange jumper?' she asked. 'You don't look like yourself at all.'

'I don't *feel* like myself,' said Dad.

'I'd take it off if I were you, and let's get you some lunch. I've had enough weirdness for one morning.'

Will followed Dad upstairs and watched as he paced back and forth in front of the clothes hamper. Three times he put his hands on the hem of the jumper and began to lift it off over his head. Three times he stopped.

'Dad,' said Will softly.

Dad blinked at him sleepily. 'Cold,' he finally said. 'Just can't bear to take this off. Can't remember why I was going to.'

Will ran back into his room.

'Here, Dad! If you're cold, try this.' He handed Dad the hat he'd just finished knitting. It had no Magic Wool in it, of course. It was just a dark green hat made of soft, thick yarn. All it had in it was Will trying to quiet his mind to get ready for Harkening Stitch – although Ivy had shown him how to knit a green leaf to attach to the top, so it looked like the top of a green bean. Will had no idea if it would help.

Dad put the hat on, looking puzzled.

'Huh. Thank you, mate. Yes, that's better.' He looked down at himself and blinked for a minute. 'Your mother's right. This is a terrible jumper.' He pulled it off over his head and dropped it into the clothes hamper, putting the hat back on as he wandered from the room.

As soon as Dad had gone downstairs Will fished the jumper back out of the hamper, using his thumb and forefingers like pincers. He lowered it into a plastic carrier bag. There. The grans would know what to do with it.

Stuffing the bag into the wire basket of his bicycle, he pedalled to The Knittery as fast as his legs would go.

17

'What fresh devilry is this?'

The grans were gathered around the table in the upstairs room at The Knittery, looking down at the flecked jumper. They were wrapped up to their chins in magical knitting, and Jun-Yu was using a pair of pliers to hold one of the sleeves up to the light.

'This looks like a generosity jumper, only . . .'

'Dicky,' said Matilda.

'Wonky,' said Hortense.

'All over the shop,' said Ivy.

'And the other sleeve – that's a happiness pattern, only . . .'

'Jump-started,' said Ivy.

'Gingered,' said Matilda.

'Sprightled up!' said Dorcas.

'And this bit round the neck looks like a wisdom jumper, only . . .'

'Is that *in reverse*?' asked Dorcas, her eyes wide.

'So it would cloud your judgement,' said Ivy.

'Look at the wrist, on the inside!' said Hortense.

'It looks like a warming jumper—' said Dorcas.

'In reverse, again,' said Jun-Yu.

'Well, that is a whole new level of scary,' said Ivy.

'So this jumper would make you *unwise*?' said Will.

'Yes. And so generous you'd spend too much money,' said Matilda.

'And weirdly cold when you took the thing off,' said Hortense.

'And miserable until you had it on again,'

breathed Dorcas.

Jun-Yu had flicked on the lamp and picked up a magnifying glass. 'Is anyone seeing any Magic Wool in here? For jumpers to work this much mischief, they'd surely *have* to have some. Will, use your young eyes.'

But Will couldn't see any more gold than the grans could.

'What are these tiny flecks?' asked Dorcas, leaning very close and running a finger over the little black bits. 'I can *feel* something here.'

Jun-Yu brought the lamp down closer, and stretched the jumper out beneath it.

'By all that's evil,' said Jun-Yu, 'I think the tiny flecks *are* Magic Wool, and he's done something to it, to stop it fighting back.'

'So it won't unravel!' said Dorcas.

'That,' said Matilda, 'is NOT cricket!'

'But they *do* unravel,' said Will. 'Ben's dad's jumper's fell to bits!'

'That's it!' said Jun-Yu. 'The Magic Wool *eventually* wins. Then it unravels, and destroys the whole jumper. But not before someone has paid for it and come to love how the jumper made them feel.'

'Then when it falls to bits, they're desperate to buy another one,' said Hortense.

'And they'll pay any price,' said Ivy.

'This is unspeakable,' said Dorcas.

'He really is a clever little blighter, isn't he?' said Matilda.

'And now he knows that Gertie was taking her family to the Isle of Man,' said Hortense. 'Do we think he'll try to go? Will he know how to find the sheep and gather the Magic Wool?'

Just then Holly swung in through the window, binoculars round her neck.

'He's gone!' she said. 'Jasper Fitchet just left Knittington on a *motorbike*. Nice one too!' Will had seen that motorbike through the binoculars. It was a Norton Dominator, the new kind that looks old but can go like the clappers.

'What are you doing up here, Holly?

Shouldn't you be manning the shop?' said Jun-Yu.

'In case you haven't noticed, we haven't had a customer for days. No one is knitting. No one is making anything. The whole town is out buying clothes.'

'But you shouldn't know about any of this, child! It's bad enough we've let Will get involved,' said Dorcas. 'These are terrible, terrible doings, and we can't let the two of you get hurt.'

'This is Mission Critical!' said Holly. 'We need every brain in the house.'

'She's right,' said Jun-Yu. 'This is a crisis. We've let it go on for far too long.' She began pacing. 'We obviously can't count on the Knitwork coming. We have to find some way to handle this ourselves.'

'Exactly! What would Gertie do?' asked Ivy.

'What would *Gertie* do?' said Holly, her nostrils flaring. 'How can you possibly know? With all due respect, Gertie never told you anything! So never mind what she would do, because we have no idea! The question is, what will *we* do?'

'It's true,' said Hortense. 'Gertie didn't give us enough to go on. She never told us enough.'

'We *have* to get some more Magic Wool,' said Jun-Yu, slapping her hand into her palm. 'We'll need it, to bring people back to themselves, and to fight whatever it is he's making. We've got to go to the Isle of Man, and we've got to find those magic sheep before the Golding Dawn.'

'Isn't that . . . tomorrow?' asked Dorcas.

'And isn't the ferry all booked up?' asked Matilda.

'We don't even have a car!' said Hortense.

For a second everyone just looked at one another.

'Come now,' said Matilda finally. 'Where's our Dunkirk spirit?'

'That's right!' said Ivy. 'Everyone stand up and let's have a few deep breaths, for inspiration.'

Everyone stood up straight and closed their eyes. Will tried not to giggle.

'Arms out in front,' said Ivy, 'and breathe! Fingers stretching wide, wide, wide as you can – and breathe! Curling into fists, tight, tight, tight as you can – and breathe! Stretching again, wide, wide, wide – and breathe! Now both hands around that invisible ball of wool, and rotate the wrists, back, forth, back, can we feel it? Are we all feeling it?'

Will had to close his eyes or he was going to laugh out loud. But as soon as he'd closed them, Will started remembering things. It was like he was watching a film. First, his own kitchen floor dropped away below him as he jumped for the first time in Dad's socks. Then the tarmac of his street moved up and down as he jumped into Holly's swinging skipping rope. And then Holly was sitting on Sophie's bed and telling that story . . .

'Hey!' he said, opening his eyes. 'The Pep-In-Your-Step socks!' The grans all blinked and looked at him. 'What if you used that pattern, only jump-started? Gingered? Sprightled up?' (*Oh, crikey!* He was starting to talk like them.) 'Could you make Seven-League Boots, like in the fairy tales? Where every step you take is three miles long, or something?'

'Well, tie me to a kite and strike me with lightning!' said Ivy.

'Sit me under a tree and pelt me with apples,' said Dorcas.

'Overfill my bath and stand by with a mop!' said Hortense.

'We *could* get there with knitting,' said Matilda.

'All right, but how do we steer?' said Ivy. 'I mean, we don't want to just walk into the sea, right?'

'How about our loo-roll cover?' said Will. He'd brought it to them to study, and they'd said it was called a Locator Hat. 'Can you use it to find a *place* instead of a thing?'

'Bless the boy! That just might work!'

'Might I suggest that everyone don her Combat Cardigan?' said Jun-Yu.

The grans all moved to a row of hooks behind the door, and each took down a patchwork cardigan. They looked a bit like the one Mum had, made of a dozen colours each, as if the grans had used the left-over bits of wool from every gift they'd knitted for the past five Christmases. Each patch seemed to be a different kind of stripe or cable or pattern of bumps.

'Combat?' asked Will. 'Against what?' To Will they looked barely organized enough to pull off just being cardigans.

'Against the Great Forgetting,' said Dorcas.

'The great . . . what?' asked Will.

'Forgetting,' said Jun-Yu.

'What's that?'

'Forgetting how to do anything for ourselves. How to make things. How to cook things. How to fix things.'

'They're great when you need ideas,' said Hortense.

'And we are going to need some of those!' said Ivy.

'And what should I do?' said Will. 'Get ready for my journey?'

'That's out of the question, Will,' said Jun-Yu. 'We can't possibly send you to the Isle of Man alone.'

'Well, then, someone come with me.'

'There won't be enough time to make boots for two, dear boy,' said Dorcas. 'This is going to be the race of our lives as it is.'

'And there might not be enough wool,' said Jun-Yu. 'Slippers this powerful will have to be knitted entirely of magic yarn. There may only be enough for a single pair.'

'I think it might be time to fetch the last of the Magic Wool from the loft,' said Dorcas.

'Quite right,' said Jun-Yu. 'That's what you can do for us, Will.'

The loft was above the kitchen behind the shop. Will held the ladder while Holly went up it, and Matilda reached up for the picnic hamper as Holly handed it down.

'Thank you, Will. Now off you go.'

'But—'

'*No*,' said Jun-Yu. 'You can ring in the morning and we'll tell you how it went.'

'Now leg it,' said Matilda.

'Sling your hook,' said Ivy.

'Off you bimble,' said Hortense.

'Get weaving,' said Dorcas.

18

The stars had all come out by the time Mum and Dad went to bed. Will hadn't been able to fall asleep. He'd watched the sky turn blue like the old glass bottles in the chemist's window, and then velvety black. He heard Mum tiptoe in and out of the bathroom, before Dad did the same, and then the click of their bedroom door closing. He heard owls hooting, and then Dad snoring. Finally he got out of bed and put his clothes on. As quietly as he could, he slid fresh batteries into his torch and put it in his rucksack.

Shoes in hand, he stole out to the upstairs hallway and into Sophie's room. Carefully, quietly, he checked the locks on the windows to make sure nothing could get in from the outside.

'Where are you going?'

'Shh. I'm not going anywhere.'

'I want to come too,' said Sophie.

'Go back to sleep, Soph,' he said softly.

He closed the door gently, crept downstairs, and slid out of the front door. He was pretty sure his parents wouldn't want him to wander outside alone at night, even to The Knittery. But there was no way he could lie in bed just waiting.

The shop was dark at the front, so Will went round to the alleyway and in through the back courtyard. The windows there were brightly lit, and the back door was unlocked. Will ducked in just as Holly was coming down the steps with a tray full of empty teacups.

'Hello, you,' she said in a low voice. 'Were you worried about them too?'

'I couldn't sleep,' said Will.

'I don't blame you,' said Holly.

'Have they made the boots?' asked Will.

'They did!' said Holly, her eyes rounding. 'It's been a twelve-hour knit-a-thon! Even my gran switched from tea to coffee.'

'Do they work?'

Holly grinned and nodded, bobbing up and down on the balls of her feet.

'They've been taking off from the courtyard,' she said, raising one leg up in front of her as if she were about to take a giant step, and making the teacups on her tray rattle. 'Jun-Yu got across the river and back, and Hortense made it up to the roof of the abbey church. Then Ivy went to Glastonbury in two steps, and Matilda's just back from crossing the Severn.'

'Woah!' said Will. 'That's way more powerful than Dad's old socks!'

'Yep!' said Holly, lowering her voice further and looking around the kitchenette as if a spy might be crouched on the draining board. 'The boots take you right where you're looking. If you want to go someplace that's too

149

far to see, you imagine the place in your mind and say something like, "Where is Portscatho Beach?" and the loo-roll cover will make you look in the right direction, just like it does when you ask where an object is.'

'What if you can't imagine it — like if you've never been there?'

'Ivy got to Blenheim Palace without ever having been before, by holding on to an old entry ticket and thinking about pictures she's seen of it. Flipped out some peacocks and set off an alarm, but no harm done.'

'It really works!'

'It does. They've got a scrap of the Magic Wool to hold on to, to help them steer to the sheep that your gran found.' She set the tray down on the counter top and put one hand on her hip. 'But I'm not sure about this whole thing. They're all too old to go chasing after sheep in the dark.' She stuffed her fingers into her hair, making one of her buns wiggle. 'Go and keep an ear on them while I wash up, OK? Sit on the stairs, so they don't see you.'

Will crept up the stairs, just far enough for his eyes to rise above the floor.

The grans were sitting in a circle in the centre of the room. On the table over by the window, Will could just make out a pair of ankle-high boots knitted in sparkling gold. Next to them lay the Dalek loo-roll cover and three empty sacks.

'There's no more wool and there's no more time,' Jun-Yu was saying. 'One pair of boots and one hat is all we've got. Whoever does this, does it alone.'

'Jun-Yu is right,' said Dorcas. 'One of us has to give it a try, and chance the ducks. The worst that can happen is that we have no luck, put on the hat and come back.'

'Actually, the worst thing that can happen is we drown in the Irish Sea . . .'

'They're trying to figure out who should go,' said Will, creeping back downstairs. He looked at Holly. 'I think they're scared.'

'Are you thinking what I'm thinking?' she asked.

'If you're thinking that one of us should go,' said Will, 'then, yes, I am.'

Holly nodded.

'I hate to say it, but I think it should be you. I think there's something important about children in all of this. That thing you remembered about your gran taking you out at dawn.' She shook her head. 'And if I'm right, then younger is probably better.' She handed Will her smartphone. 'The shop is number two on speed dial. Jun-Yu is number three. And you know about 999, right?'

Will nodded.

'I'll distract them. You swipe the boots and the hat, and don't forget the bit of wool. When you put the hat on, try to think of the picture you saw on your gran's computer — the one of her with the sheep. Hopefully that will take you to wherever it was that she got the wool last time.' Holly stared at Will for a second, biting her bottom lip.

'Sound action stations!' Will whispered.

Holly smiled. 'We shall beat to quarters!'

'What does that even mean?' said Will.

Holly strode up the stairs two at a time. 'Hey!' she said loudly. 'I've got a question!'

Will tiptoed behind her, stopping on the second-from-the-top step with his legs under him, like a sprinter waiting for the starting shot. He watched Holly's feet crossing the floorboards, and then put his chin above the floor so he could see more. All the grans were looking at Holly. Which meant they weren't looking at the staircase, or the table with the hat and boots on it.

'Should I make up a flask and some sandwiches for whoever is going to do this?' Holly was asking. 'Because we don't know how cold it might be on the Isle of Man, and we don't know how long it's going to take.'

As silently as he could, Will scuttled to the table.

'And what about torches? Should I dig around and find some?'

He tugged the hat on, scooped up the boots and the bags and the little bit of yarn, then crept back down the stairs, careful not to let the boards creak beneath his feet.

'And I'm just wondering if Google Maps could help at all?' Holly was saying. 'I could show you how to use it.'

Will slipped out into the courtyard, between the roses and the wheelie bins. The night was silent except for the murmur of voices coming from the window above.

He sat down on the mossy brick ground and stuffed the three empty bags into his rucksack. Then he put the boots on. They were more like slippers than boots, and they stretched easily over his trainers. Careful not to take a step, he stood up slowly.

What next? He should concentrate on the Isle of Man, he supposed. Closing his eyes, he imagined the pictures he'd seen on Gran's laptop: seals and thatched white crofts, and Gran with the four-horned sheep. When he had the pictures firmly in his mind, he whispered, 'Where is the Isle of Man?' then opened his eyes to let the Locator Hat direct his gaze. He felt a pull at his eyes, and his face followed. Next he would need to take a step in that direction.

What if I land in the ocean, though?

He was just working up the nerve to lift his left foot when there was a sudden eruption of voices from the upstairs window.

'Wait – Stop! – What are you doing, child? – Oh, no!'

He mustn't turn his head. Quickly! He had to step, and he had to do it now.

He raised his left foot in the air, pointing in the direction of his gaze, and pushed off with his right leg as hard as he could.

Something heavy thumped him on his back, knocking him forward. Before he could catch his breath, a blast of icy wind chilled his face and almost blew the Locator Hat off. It sounded like the engine of an aeroplane. His eyes blurred, his stomach lurched, and the soles of his feet tickled. He glimpsed dark, silvered water beneath him and then felt soft ground under his left foot. He fell on to his knees in a patch of tall, dark grass. A second later his rucksack landed hard against his back, knocking him on to his face.

Only then it scrambled off him again.

'Sorry!' It wasn't his rucksack at all.

'Sophie!'

He rolled over and sat up in the grass. Sophie was standing above him, wearing a jumper over her pyjamas, her Kitty Hat on her head, and her red wellies on her feet.

Pants! Now he was going to be in more trouble than ever.

'How did you get here?'

'I did the flying mount,' she said, grinning. So that was what had thumped him so hard on the back just as he was stepping off.

'You followed me out of the house?' Will asked.

'Cronk said I should.'

'And all the way to The Knittery?'

Sophie smiled and nodded. 'And then I jumped up and held on to your rucksack!' The grans would be having kittens. They'd have seen it all from the window.

'You really shouldn't have, Sophie. That could have gone badly.'

'I want to help get the golden wool,'

she said. She must have heard more than they'd thought. Well, she'd have to come along now.

Will looked around. They were in a meadow alongside a huddle of small white cottages. As his eyes adjusted to the darkness, the moonlight showed him their thatched roofs and low doorways. It was a tiny village, like the one in the picture on Gran's computer. There was no sound except the noises of animals: night birds hunting and mice rustling. If there were people in this village, they were all sleeping.

Will pulled the knitted boots off and stowed them in his rucksack. He took out Holly's phone. Only one bar showed in the upper corner. He pressed 3 for Jun-Yu.

'Will! Is that . . . ank heavens! . . . ophie?' Jun-Yu sounded very fuzzy and far away.

'Yes!' said Will. 'I have Sophie. I think we're at the village where Gran got the wool.'

'. . . ear me? I can't . . . there?'

'I have SOPHIE,' said Will slowly. 'We're on

the ISLE of MAN.'

'. . . ow listen . . . I want you to put those boots . . . back home . . .'

'I can't hear you,' said Will.

'. . . right now!'

'CAN'T HEAR YOU,' said Will. 'We'll be back soon, I promise!'

'Will . . . and . . . ediately!'

And then there was nothing. Will put the phone back into the rucksack. At least the grans knew they'd made it.

'Look at the stars, Will!' said Sophie.

They both tilted their heads back.

'Wow!' said Will. He hadn't realized so many stars even existed. 'Lucky it's such a clear night,' he said. There were no street-lights. Will wasn't sure there was even any street. 'I wonder where we go next.'

He was just considering whether the loo-roll cover might be any help with that, when Sophie suddenly squeaked, 'That cat just talked to me!'

'What?'

'That cat there.' Sophie pointed. In the shadow, under the overhanging thatch of one of the crofts, sat a very large tabby cat. As they watched, it stood up and stretched its front legs, then slowly walked towards them.

'Can you hear it talking?' asked Sophie. Will shook his head.

'It just said, "Good evening".'

The cat came and rubbed itself against her boots. Like Cronk, it had no tail.

'Maybe it's because of my Kitty Hat,' said Sophie.

Of course! The hat was probably magic.

'Sophie, could I just borrow it?'

Sophie looked at him with one eyebrow raised. Will wished he could do that.

'You want to wear my *Kitty Hat*?' she asked.

'Please.'

Sophie took it off and handed it to him. Will handed her the toilet-roll cover. He watched to make sure she put it on firmly. Now he'd be able to see where it was at all times.

The Kitty Hat was a bit small for him, but he managed to squeeze it on. Instantly, he heard a low, smooth voice in his head.

'You don't happen to be carrying any food, do you?'

Will almost screamed. The cat was looking right up into his face.

'Because you'll have scared off the mice, you know.'

'Oh, I'm sorry.' Will searched his pockets. 'Do you like peanuts? I've got a handful of those.'

The cat sauntered up to Will and sniffed his hand. 'Mmm. No, I don't think so,' it said, giving its paw a shake and sitting back on its tail-less rump. 'How is my brother?'

'Your brother?'

'Yes. You're from the old woman, aren't you? The one who came and got fleece here and took my brother, back when I was a kitten. Your jumper smells of her.'

'Do you mean Cronk?' said Will. 'Is this

where Cronk came from? Sophie, this is Cronk's brother!'

'Sister,' said the cat. 'But whatever.'

'You are lovely-lovely-lovely and I love you!' said Sophie, bending down and scratching behind the cat's ears.

'Cronk's living with us now, since Gran died,' said Will. 'Sophie, is Cronk happy?'

'Yes, he likes all our beds,' said Sophie.

'Will you take him a message for me?' asked the cat.

'Of course!' said Will.

'Will you tell him: *Ta fys ayd c'wooad ta my ghraih ort.*'

'*What?*' said Will.

The cat stared at him. 'You don't understand Manx?' If the cat had been a person, Will was pretty sure she would have rolled her eyes. 'Just tell him *Hi.*'

'Hey,' said Will, 'you wouldn't happen to know where to find a herd of magic sheep? The kind my gran was after?'

'The ones your gran used are over there,'

said the cat, pointing with her nose towards a nearby fence. 'But they're like pets. There are better ones on the other side of the hill there.'

'Better ones?'

'More wild. They eat brush plants, so they turn more golden. That's what you're after, isn't it?'

'Yes!' said Will. 'Exactly!'

'Over the hill, across the lane, over the stile, and through the trees. If you fall in the sea you've gone too far.'

The cat trotted off across the grass, like a fur-covered shadow.

'Thanks!' called Will softly.

Of course, the Locator Hat wouldn't work for them now, since these were different sheep. But he had directions from the cat. He laughed softly. If you'd told him a month ago that he'd be looking for a herd of magic sheep following advice from a cat . . .

'Has that ever happened to you before,

Soph?' Will asked as they walked towards the hill. 'That you could hear a cat talking when you were wearing your Kitty Hat?'

'I keep telling you!' said Sophie. 'I can hear Cronk.' So she'd been telling the truth.

'But no other cats?'

'Only that one.'

'Hmm,' said Will. 'So maybe this is a *Manx* Kitty Hat.'

They were quiet as they pumped themselves up the side of the hill.

'I can see the sea!' said Sophie as they came to the top. Far off, beyond Sophie's pointing finger, moonlight made a white path on the glinting black water. In front of them, the hill sloped down into tree-shaded darkness.

Just as the cat had said, they came to a lane at the bottom of the hill, and then went over a stile. Will switched his torch on as the trees closed overhead. The path was wide and clear, but pitch black. The leaves whispered above them, and there was a smell of wet sticks and salad.

When they came out of the trees they could see the sea again, even closer now. There was a breeze on Will's face. The path looked white and the grass grey. The sky was changing from black to deep blue.

'I don't see anything yet,' said Will. His feet were tired, he'd eaten all the peanuts, and pricky-sticky gorse and thistles scratched his ankles. He was impressed that Sophie hadn't complained.

The sky was lightening gently as they walked, the grass turning from grey to green. Birds began singing from every corner of the meadow.

'What's that sound?' asked Sophie.

Will stopped. He could hear it too. A soft *meh-eh-eh-eh*. Suddenly Sophie grabbed Will's sleeve. 'Will, look!'

The edge of the sky was glowing with the first light of dawn. Where a moment before there had been nothing but shadow and scrub, they could now see sheep spread before them along the slope. Some were standing up, some were lying down, and some were staring at Will and Sophie.

All of them were gold.

20

'Blimey!' said Will. Was it just the pinken-ing sky and the early sun? Every one of the sheep was sparkling.

Will and Sophie ran a few steps closer. It was as if the insides of a treasure chest had been spread all across the grass. The sheep were soft brown, the colour of walnut coffee cake, but tipped with sparkling rose gold, like Mum and Dad's wedding rings. Each one had four horns, two on either side. Some of them curled down by their ears, others stuck straight up in the air.

'They look prehistoric,' said Will.

'They're lovely-lovely-lovely and I *love*

them!' said Sophie. 'I want to squeeze them!'

'Go on, then. I dare you!' said Will.

Sophie ran forward and dived at the nearest sheep, which bobbed off just out of reach. *Meh-eh-eh-eh.* The other sheep rippled away.

'*Roaw! Roaw!*' An echoing bark sounded from somewhere to the left. Will swung his head round. A large white shape was bounding towards them across the thistled slope. '*Roaw! Roaw!*'

'Dog!' said Sophie, and clapped her hands.

It looked more like a polar bear to Will. Only it was faster. And it was growling.

'Sophie,' said Will, trying to keep his voice steady, 'we've got to get out of here.' He'd already pulled his rucksack round and unzipped it to search for the slipper-boots.

But Sophie laughed.

'No, we don't!' she said. 'I have a juckie in my pocket.' She did, of course. 'As long as I squeeze it when I meet them, dogs just think I'm the boss dog.' Before Will could stop her, Sophie stepped out towards the dog, left hand in her pocket, right hand extended.

'Good boy! Good boy! What sort of doggie are you, then?'

'Sophie, no!' said Will, plunging forward to grab her, just as the giant thing stopped in front of them. It was so close Will could smell dog breath. It rolled over on to the grass with its feet in the air.

'I'll scratch your stomach, shall I?' said Sophie, walking up to it and reaching down to scratch the dog's white underbelly. 'Good boy. Good boy. I think you are a Great Peer-a-knees.'

Will's heart started working again. It was true, then: Sophie's knitted juckies were magic too. Sophie was giggling and pounding the sides of the dog's huge chest. The dog's paws were curled over coyly, and its tongue was lolling out of its mouth.

Finally the dog rolled back over and stood on its feet, giving itself a shake. Sophie only came up as high as its back, and it stood nearly eye to eye with Will. Its massive tail swept back and forth like an industrial feather duster.

'I'm glad you had your Gran-dog, Soph.'

Will looked round them. The sheep had cleared away when the dog had come, and they were surrounded by sheep-less scrub. How were they going to get any fleece if the sheep just ran away when you got near them?

But then the sun rose a centimetre higher, lighting the ground around them, and Will saw that the thorns and thistles were covered with sparkling golden wool.

'Sophie! It's Fluff-in-the Faddle! Let's race!'

Quickly, carefully, they picked bits of fluff from the pointy leaves around their feet, and stuffed it into the bags. When they'd hoovered up everything nearby they spread out over the meadow, and then to the brambles in the hedge where it clung like golden snow. Their fingers got pricked and their clothes got stuck, but they kept going. When the three bags were full, they stuffed fleece into Will's rucksack, and into the little rucksack that Sophie wore on her back. Finally they had as much fleece as they could carry.

'We should get back.' Will couldn't imagine what time it must be.

'I love you, sheepies!' Sophie called.

'Thank you, er, sheepies,' said Will, putting his rucksack on his front to make room for Sophie on his back. 'Now, Soph, I'm going to put the slippers on. I want you to keep the hat on until you've jumped up, and then put it on my head when you're on my back. Just to make sure I don't accidentally step off without you.'

'Who's that?' asked Sophie.

'Oh pants!' said Will.

Heading towards them across the field was a person. Farmers got up at dawn, Will remembered. He and Sophie were probably trespassing. Did these sheep belong to someone?

Will looked around quickly. 'Let's try for those trees over there.'

They ran across the grass to the edge of the wood, and Will put the slippers on. Then he turned his back and crouched low.

'OK, Soph. Flying mount! And then put the hat on my head!'

He waited to feel the thump on his back. It didn't come. Instead he heard Sophie squeal. Will's heart skipped four beats, and then gave a massive pound as he whirled around to see Sophie in the air, tucked under the arm of Jasper Fitchet.

21

'Don't move,' said the man, his wolf-tail eyebrows drawn together fiercely. 'Either of you!'

'What do you want?' asked Will, hoping he sounded braver than he felt. He wasn't at all sure that Fitchet wouldn't hurt Sophie.

'Let's start with those bags of wool. Put them down on the grass here and then step backwards – further. There's a good chap. Now, let's have you kneel down so you won't run off – yes, good – and let's have those slippers you were about to put on. Why don't you make them into a ball for me? – you know how, I'm sure – nice and toss-able.

Good. Now if you'll use an easy underarm throw and – OW!'

Sophie had bitten him. A second later she was running.

'Sophie! Catch!' Will tossed her the balled-up boots and dived at Jasper Fitchet's knees. It wasn't what you'd call an elegant tackle, but the man fell and Will gripped him round his legs. For a second he saw stars, but when his eyes cleared he could see Sophie still running, her little backpack bobbing.

'Sophie, go! Put the slippers on!' Will shouted.

Mr Fitchet was kicking hard and his sharp knees were digging into Will's chest. He couldn't hold on much longer. But Sophie had dropped to the ground and pulled the slippers on over her wellies.

'Think of the grans! Think of The Knittery!'

Just then Fitchet managed to wriggle free. He lunged towards Sophie, who was standing still with her eyes squeezed shut. Her head swung round and she took a step towards the man's open arms. He dived for her, but found himself grabbing thin air. With a rush of wind, Sophie had disappeared.

Will's heart started beating again. At least Sophie was safe. *And one rucksack of wool has made it to the grans,* he thought.

'You disappoint me, Will.' Mr Fitchet was panting, his muddy hands hanging at his side, his trouser knees torn. 'Someone as clever as you should never have to stoop to violence.' He pulled a white linen handkerchief from his pocket and wiped mud from his hands. 'We could work together, you know. It would be much the best solution. I could use an apprentice.'

'An apprentice worm?' asked Will. 'An assistant swindler?'

'You'd rather make baby toys and tea cosies, would you?' Jasper chuckled. 'That's for grannies. You and I can do better.'

'Making ugly fake clothes that fall apart?'

'People will buy ugly clothes that fall apart whether I make them or not. Why shouldn't they buy ugly clothes made in Knittington by me!' He chuckled again. 'Buy local!'

'But you're making people forget who they are. They forget how to do anything when they're wearing your jumpers. All they do is shop and get sad.'

'They're doing that anyway.'

'But why not use all of this magic you've discovered to make things better, instead of getting better at being a nasty-jack?'

The man pressed his thin lips into a little grin and shook his big white forehead. 'You can't fight the world, my boy. It's way bigger than us. I might as well make money out of it instead of the next fellow. How about ten per cent, Will? Just for your promise to help? Wouldn't your family like a better house? How about a BMX?'

It was true about the house, of course. Mum and Dad were always worrying about the rising damp and the leaking roof and the pre-historic plumbing.

'But the wool doesn't like it. The wool doesn't *want* you to do those things,' said Will.

'Wool doesn't *want*, Will. You just have to take control. You can get used to that sick feeling – I know you've discovered it by now. It stops hurting after a while.'

But Will didn't want to get used to that feeling. Then he'd be like Mr Fitchet. And he didn't want anyone else's mum and dad to ever look like his mum and dad had when they were wearing those jumpers. Especially if they didn't have Gran's knitting to help snap them out of it.

'No, thank you,' said Will. 'Gran didn't like what you were up to, and I guess she knew what she was on about.'

'You think your precious gran was so good?' asked Fitchet. 'Why didn't she tell you anything? Why didn't she teach you? And the rest of that lot, they haven't told you the half of it, boy. Have they told you anything about the Knitwitch?'

'Well,' said Will, 'I know that she's the leader.'

'The Knitwitch wants to keep all the power for herself,' said Fitchet. 'Well, fine. You can stay scared and ignorant and keep to your place, but I won't. We could have been very helpful to one another, Will. But it's nothing to me. You've just given me enough wool for a year, anyway.' He picked up the woolsacks.

From down the slope came a sound like a hurricane beating against a window. Or was it barking? A horse-shaped blur shot out of the trees.

'*Raow! Raow!*' It was the giant dog. The Great Thing-a-knees. It bounded towards Fitchet like the night train to Aberdeen.

Ka-thump!

The dog's front paws landed on the man's chest, knocking him and the bags of wool to the ground.

Will plunged for the bags, wrenching them away from Fitchet. Slinging them up over his shoulders, he ran.

'Thank you!' he called, the bags bumping crazily as he ran. 'Thank you, Thing-a-knees!'

22

Down the slope, over a gate and out across another field Will charged, flying through gorse and heather, jumping over streams. He didn't look back. Only when he couldn't go any further did he stop. Heaving for breath, he dropped the bags and looked around him. He was in a meadow full of tall grass and dragonflies. There was no sign of Jasper Fitchet.

Still panting, Will took the phone from his pocket. There was no signal. Maybe Sophie had found the grans, and someone could use the boots and hat to find him. Maybe one of them was on her way now. But he had no way of knowing.

There was a narrow, unpaved lane at the bottom of the meadow. Will slung the bags of wool back over his shoulders and began walking towards it. He'd only gone a few steps when a faint roar burst out from the direction of the lane. It was the sound of a small engine, like a lawn mower . . . an old motorbike. A second roar joined it. Will ran towards it.

As he reached the lane, two of the strangest contraptions Will had ever seen pulled up. One was an Enfield Bullet with knobbly tyres and a sidecar that looked like a piece of a very old aeroplane, the sides painted with flames. The other was a BSA Gold Scrambler. Its sidecar looked like a large basket, with a bale of hay in place of a seat. Each bike had a sparkly golden slipper over one of its handgrips, and both bikes were covered with grans! Grans riding pillion, grans stuffed into sidecars. They were wearing open-faced helmets and goggles, waving

their arms and yelling.

'Will!' The engines puttered and the motor-cycles stopped alongside the stone wall lining the lane. There was a huge cheer as Will clambered to the top of the wall with the bags of wool.

'Hurrah!'

'Woo hoo!' called Ivy as the engines died

down. She was sitting behind Matilda on the Bullet, waving the loo-roll cover. 'I haven't had so much fun in donkey's years!' She was the only one not wearing a helmet.

'Is Sophie OK?'

'Home asleep by now,' said Matilda, 'though it was sticky wickets sneaking her back into your house!'

'We made Holly do it!' said Hortense.

'Fortunately we'd gone to get the motorbikes as soon as we saw you leave,' said Jun-Yu, her face becoming stern. 'You naughty, wicked, mischievous, reckless—'

'It's a jammy thing I keep my motorbike ready to ride,' said Ivy, 'just for sentimental reasons!'

'And lucky my granddaughters are a bunch of rip-tackle tomboys who've kept the old farm bike up so they can back-racket round the fields,' said Dorcas.

'And you put the Seven-League Slippers over the handgrips!' said Will. He should try that out on his bike.

'Then Ivy put the Locator Hat on to steer and stood with one foot on each bike as we rode.'

'*What?*' said Will.

'Don't lose your onion, old bean,' said Matilda, picking up one of the woolsacks. 'Ivy's top-hole at motorbike tricks.' She tossed the bag to Hortense.

'Oof!' said Hortense, falling backwards on to the grass.

'A little less enthusiasm there, Matilda dear,' said Jun-Yu.

'That way we could get both bikes here,' Ivy explained. 'In case you needed reinforcements.'

'Right!' said Jun-Yu. 'Everyone ready to get back?'

'What, and not ride just a little bit of the TT course while we're here?' said Ivy.

'This is no time for larking about,' said Jun-Yu. 'We've got to get Will home before his parents wake up! Are you up for doing your trick again?'

Ivy gave a thumbs-up. 'Everything cushti!'

Will noticed a far-off rumble. Another motorbike was coming.

'Bandits! Bandits!' said Hortense, who was standing next to him. 'Two o'clock!'

The grans stood up like meerkats, staring into the distance.

It was a Norton Dominator.

'It's Fitchet!' Will cried.

'Ankle it!' said Matilda.

'Blues and twos!' said Hortense.

They all piled on to the motorbikes, with Will in the sidecar of the Bullet next to one of the woolsacks. 'Hold on tight!' said Matilda, and started the engine. It was like sitting on a pneumatic drill. Next to them, Hortense started the Scrambler and then helped get Dorcas on in the driver's position. Jun-Yu climbed into the Scrambler's sidecar with the other two bags of wool, while Ivy clambered up behind Matilda to sit sideways, with both legs on the right side of the bike.

'Tally ho!' called Hortense.

The Scrambler pulled off with a roar and a puff of dust. The Bullet followed, springing down the rocky lane. Will clutched the edges of the sidecar to keep from being thrown out of the back. He looked over his shoulder. It was definitely Jasper Fitchet. He was close enough that Will could see the man's little grin, pressed more tightly than ever as he hunched over the handlebars of the Dominator.

'*Go! Go! Go!*' shouted Will above the racket of the engine.

The grans' bikes picked up speed, curving round bends. Will looked back again. Jasper's bike was powerful, but it couldn't handle the gravel and grass like the Scrambler and it was no match for the Bullet's knobbly tyres. His handlebars swerved, and he slowed down. Meanwhile, the grans' bikes barely wobbled on the loose road surface, though the bags of wool bounced whenever they hit a dip or a bump, and they would have fallen out at one point if Will and Jun-Yu hadn't grabbed hold of them. The distance between the grans and Jasper Fitchet widened.

The lane twisted again and then finally joined a proper road, wide enough to get the bikes next to one another. The Scrambler pulled out on to the tarmac and the Bullet followed. Slowly the Bullet crept up alongside the Scrambler, the engine rumbling more loudly than ever, until they were side by side, the Bullet on the left and the Scrambler on the right.

But by now, the Dominator had reached the tarmac too, and the distance between them was shrinking again. Jasper Fitchet was grinning widely, his eyebrows knitted together.

'He's getting closer!' yelled Will.

Up behind Matilda, Ivy put the Dalek loo-roll cover on her head. Holding on to Matilda's shoulder with her left hand, she stood up on the right pillion peg of the Scrambler.

'Don't fall!' yelled Jun-Yu, clutching the

bags as they bounced against the back of the sidecar.

They were coming into a town now, and the edges of the road were already lined with spectators. There must be a race this morning, and people had come early for a good spot. It was lucky they hadn't closed the road yet, thought Will.

A huge cheer went up as Ivy stood straight, her silver plaits flying, and put her right arm and leg out into the air, stretching towards the Scrambler.

'It's the White Helmets!' came cries from the crowd.

'It's the Motomaids!'

Ivy waved and smiled then slowly stepped across the gap, her right foot landing on the peg of the Scrambler's sidecar.

'Hurrah!' screamed the crowd as Ivy stretched out in an X shape between the two bikes.

Will peeked under his arm again. Jasper Fitchet was centimetres behind them, his wheel beginning to edge in between the two bikes, as if he wanted to drive them apart. Leaning forward, he took his hand off the left handgrip and reached towards Will.

'Woo hoo!' yelled Ivy. 'Where is—'

Fitchet lurched forward and grabbed a fluttering corner of Will's woolsack.

'No!' shouted Will, and gave an almighty tug on the bag. It flew out of Fitchet's grip and thumped Matilda on the back. The Bullet only swerved for a second before Matilda had it under control again, but that was all it took. Ivy wobbled, her arms waving. Will and Jun-Yu both swooped to steady her, letting go of the sacks. The bags of wool seemed to sail off the back of the bike in slow motion through the air. Will looked behind him in time to see them hitting Jasper Fitchet in the chest before everything went blurry.

The side of Will's face was struck with a freezing blast of air, and his fingers, clutching the rim of the sidecar, felt like someone was whacking them with an ice hammer.

Then they hit tarmac. Matilda braked so hard that the back wheel lifted up and the whole bike nearly went over. Beside them the Scrambler skidded sideways and stopped in front of the Bullet. Ivy soared towards the sky and came down to land in a hedge, turning a somersault as she went.

The grans all tumbled off the bikes and rushed to the hedge.

'Are you all right, Ivy?'

Ivy sat up, laughing. 'That was terrific!' she cried.

'Are you injured?'

'I think I've broken four legs!' she said. 'Did we make it?'

'We made it!'

They were on a familiar lane. The tower of Knittington Abbey rose up above the trees just ahead.

'Fitchet got our wool!' said Will.

'Pipped at the post!' said Hortense.

But nothing was going to dampen the grans' moods today.

'Never mind,' said Jun-Yu. 'We've still got some in Sophie's rucksack.'

'I've got a bit in mine too,' said Will.

Jun-Yu and Hortense were helping lift Dorcas off the bike. 'I haven't had so much fun since the last millennium!'

'Brings it all back, doesn't it?' said Matilda.

'Wait,' said Will. 'Were you guys actually . . . the *Motomaids*?'

'Hmm . . . well, you might well *think* so,' said Hortense.

'We couldn't possibly say,' said Matilda, laughing.

'Don't believe a word of it!' said Ivy, winking.

Will was disappointed not to go all the way home by motorbike, but he had to agree with Jun-Yu that the noise would not help him sneak in un-noticed. They let him off at the end of the alleyway, and he slipped through the back door seconds before Dad ambled downstairs, yawning.

'Wow, I've slept late!' he said, stretching. 'And it's Open Day at the museum tomorrow. I'd better get a move on with my lecture – and see if I can drum up some volunteers.' He was still worried, Will knew.

They found Sophie asleep on the living-room sofa in her muddy pyjamas and red wellies. 'What on earth have you two been up to?' asked Dad, looking from Sophie to Will. 'Is that *gorse* in your hair?'

'We woke up really, really early,' said Will. 'And we didn't want to wake you so we, er, went to play outside.' It was more or less true.

'Well,' said Dad, scratching his head, 'let's get you some breakfast.'

Once Mum had decided that neither of them had a fever, no one seemed to mind that Will and Sophie went back to bed after their scrambled eggs.

23

Ding-dong.

Will's eyes snapped open. The wool. The grans! *Sophie?*

He scrambled out of bed and ran to Sophie's room. She sat up in bed and yawned, surrounded by stuffed dogs. Phew!

'Someone's at the door,' she said.

Ding-dong.

It was Holly. She was standing on the front path holding a dripping rucksack.

'I stole the fleece,' she said.

'You *what*?' asked Will.

'Hello, Holly!' Dad came out of the study. 'I'm glad to see you're awake, Will. We were starting to worry.'

Dad let Holly put her rucksack in the kitchen sink while he made sandwiches. 'Is it OK if I take Will and Sophie out on a mission?' Holly asked.

'Yes, that's fine, if you want to,' Dad said. 'But you've all got to eat some lunch first.' Fortunately there was no more kale salad.

'But what are we *doing* on this mission?' asked Will, when Dad went up to get Sophie.

'It's like Sleeping Beauty's castle over at The Knittery,' said Holly, grabbing a sandwich from the plate. 'They put the fleece in a basin to soak, put the kettle on to boil, and then just fell asleep, from the looks of it.'

'They're going to bust a gasket when they wake up and find the fleece gone,' said Will, peeling the top of a sandwich up and looking inside suspiciously.

'Serves them right!' said Holly. 'I can't *believe* they took the Scrambler to the Isle of Man and didn't take me!' She swallowed. 'You're safe. It's just cheese and pickle,' she said. 'Anyway, we haven't got time to waste! There's a lot to do before they can knit with that wool.'

'Really?' asked Will, closing his eyes and taking a bite. *Ahh.* Regular old cheddar, just like Gran's.

'Really,' said Holly. 'It's got to be washed and carded and spun. So there's no time for gadling.'

'A still bee gathers no honey,' Will said.

'Oh, crikey, we *both* sound like them now!'

Dad had to work on his Open Day stuff after lunch, and Mum was filling out job applications, so they didn't mind if Will went to the river with Holly. Of course, Sophie wanted to come too. 'Cronk said I should.'

'Oh, well, if *Cronk* says you should . . .' said Will, chuckling. But then he remembered.

'Actually,' said Holly. 'If Cronk says she should . . .'

'Right,' said Will.

They went to the riverbank just downstream from Jasper Fitchet's factory. Will stopped to look through the windows with Holly's binoculars. The shop was closed, the factory windows dark, the car park empty. There was no sign of a Norton Dominator. However fast Jasper Fitchet's fancy motorbike was, it wasn't as fast as Seven-League Slippers. Maybe the grans would win after all. Maybe they could make something to stop him before he got back with the bags of Magic Wool.

It was a warm day, and they were all glad to get their feet into the cold river. The grans had put the fleece into mesh bags, like the ones Mum used to wash her tights. Holly said to sway the bags back and forth under the water, so the current could run through. Soon it became a game, trying to walk through the river on the mossy stones without slipping, while sweeping the fleece back and forth.

Even without the skipping rope, Holly was a fun magnet. Whatever she was doing, somehow she always made you want to do it too. It wasn't long before Isabelle and Robyn turned up, and then Vivien and Finn, and then Olive and Annie and Ivan and Alexi. Soon they were passing the bags back and forth and splashing each other and then falling in and swimming, and it was only because Will had tied his bag to his wrist that he didn't lose his share of the Magic Wool.

'We should spread it on a lawn next,' said Holly, wringing out Sophie's T-shirt. Everyone else had gone home to get dry.

'Where?' asked Will.

'At my house,' said Holly. 'He can't see it from the factory.'

She took them on her bicycle, with Sophie in the basket saying, 'Faster! faster!' and Will on the back, each of them holding their bag of fleece up in the air. The fleece looked just as beautiful spread out on the grass behind Holly's farmhouse as it had on the Isle of Man. It glittered when the sun came out from behind the clouds.

'Right!' said Holly when she'd pedalled them back. 'You let me know if you see anything from your window, and I'll let you know when this stuff is dry.'

24

The next morning Dad and Mum literally bumped into each other in the kitchen.

'We've got to find a craftsperson!' Dad was saying into his phone, reaching for the bread. 'Historic Crafts are on the schedule.'

'So you need to find a teacher,' Mum was saying into *her* phone, reaching for the tea tin. 'That drawing class has to run.'

'Well, check, then. I'll be there in ten minutes,' said Dad, shooting towards the refrigerator.

'I'll check,' said Mum. 'I'll ring you back in five.' She dived for the kettle.

Bam!

'Oh! Darling, I'm sorry!' said Mum.

'No! Darling, my fault!' said Dad.

'You wouldn't be able to take Will and Sophie to work with you for an hour or two this morning, would you?' asked Mum, rubbing her forehead where it had bumped Dad's chin.

'Today? It's the Open Day!' said Dad, rubbing his chin where it had bumped Mum's forehead.

'Yes, of course,' said Mum. 'It's just that the drawing teacher hasn't shown up to the summer school, and they'll pay really well if I can step in for him—'

'Yes, of course,' said Dad. 'It's just that our blacksmith hasn't shown up for the demonstration, and the museum inspector lady's coming, and if anything goes wrong today—'

'Don't worry. You just get going,' said Mum. 'Goodbye!'

'Good luck!'

'Get out!'

Dad ran up the front path with a tie in one

pocket and a sandwich in the other. Mum shut the door and began dialling her phone. The doorbell rang.

'Can Will and Sophie play?' It was Holly.

'I love you, Holly!' said Mum. She grabbed Holly's hand and put some money in it from the basket in the hall. 'I'll be back at noon!'

Mum ran up the front path, with an apple in one pocket and a bundle of drawing pencils in the other.

'I guess that means yes,' said Holly.

'Are the grans OK?' asked Will.

'The grans are in their Combat Cardigans, unravelling everything in sight.'

'They're *unravelling* magic knitting? Even *Gran's* magic knitting?'

'Yep. They say they're going to need every bit of Magic Wool we've got.' She paused. 'They're inventing something new.'

'They're *inventing* a pattern? A *new* pattern?'

'Cometh the hour, cometh the gran,' said Holly. 'They've even agreed that we should do the carding and the spinning of the new wool. It's dry now, by the way.'

'They're letting *us* take over?' asked Will.

'Uh-huh,' said Holly, bobbing up on the balls of her feet with a smug smile. 'Apparently we did all the right things yesterday.' Her face got serious. 'But today is a whole different ball game. I don't suppose you know anyone who can help us card and spin?'

Will laughed. 'Every kid in Knittington knows how to spin! At least if they've had Gran as a supply teacher!' Gran's speciality had been teaching the children to spin with drop spindles, and then, once they had their hands busy, reading them stories. They had held contests to see who could spin the most by the end of the story.

'Does it matter if it's bumpy and uneven?' asked Will.

'It only matters that it's fast,' said Holly.

'We can have a race!' said Will.

'Brilliant!' said Holly.

'Cronk says to find the spindles,' said Sophie.

Will was puzzled. 'What spindles, Sophie?'

'The ones Grandad made for Gran.' She was wearing the loo-roll cover on her head.

They didn't even laugh. Instead Will and Holly followed Sophie down the back garden and out into the alley.

'What are you up to? Can we come?' It was Olive and Annie. Soon they were following, along with Clara and Marius, Henry and Jacob, Finn and Vivien, and Rafi with all his brothers. Sophie skipped along at the front, leading them up to the back gates of the museum.

'Oh, I remember!' said Will, as they crunched over the white pebbles of the court-yard. 'Gran used to demonstrate wool crafts here sometimes.' There was a box of her old spindles and carding combs under the stairs. The spindles all had little animal heads carved on them.

Dad wasn't in his office, but there seemed to be a crowd in the gift shop. Will slipped inside. It was full of people with big cameras and name-tags saying PRESS. Dad was behind the ticket counter with the museum director, looking pale.

'We've got half an hour to come up with a family-friendly demonstration of traditional crafts,' the director was saying under her breath. 'Think!'

'Hey, Dad! Could we use the carding combs and spindles under the stairs? We're having a carding and spinning race!'

For a second Dad and the director stared.

'I love you, Will,' said the director.

'I think that means yes,' said Dad, smiling.

It was a smashing morning. The children all got their pictures in the *Knitton-Perlham Gazette*, with Sophie wearing the loo-roll cover, under the headline: DYING CRAFTS REVIVED AT LOCAL MUSEUM. The Wool Merchant's House got ninety-one points out of a hundred from the museum inspector, and the grans got metres and metres of strong, bumpy yarn the colour of coffee walnut cake, glittering with gold.

25

'Is that the new secret weapon?' asked Will.

He was upstairs at The Knittery. Jun-Yu and Dorcas were sitting at either side of the table. In between them lay what looked like an enormously long, narrow scarf. They were each knitting one end of it, their fingers moving like quick birds.

'We're calling it a Dispelling Scarf,' said Jun-Yu, without looking up.

'To gently unravel tangles, knots and hexes, and undo the work of troubled souls,' said Dorcas, her fingers flying.

'We're hoping it will free the Magic Wool from whatever Mr Fitchet has done to it,' said Dorcas.

'We're going to wrap it round the factory,' said Jun-Yu.

'Wow!' said Will. 'It's going to have to be a really long scarf to fit round the whole building. Couldn't we just wrap it around him?'

'I don't want any of us to go near him,' said Jun-Yu. 'The man is dangerous. If we can avoid seeing him or any of his diabolical jumpers, we'll have a much better chance of succeeding.'

'Besides, if we can get it around the whole factory, it should un-knit whatever devilishness he's got in there,' said Dorcas.

'Will he still be able to make more magic afterwards?'

'Yes,' said Jun-Yu. 'It won't change his abilities. But it will save our town from his diabolical clothes, at least for the moment.'

'Hm,' said Will. He wasn't sure. 'How about using Harkening Stitch?'

'That's just what your gran would have done,' said Jun-Yu, with a sad little smile.

'But Harkening Stitch works best when you do it for yourself. If we could make Mr Fitchet knit some – even just a few inches – that could do the trick.' She sighed. 'But I can't picture *that* happening.'

'Try not to worry, Will,' said Dorcas. She held the strand of yarn out to him. 'Feel this.' Will took it in his fingers and rolled it back and forth. His fingertips tingled. 'Never felt anything like it in all my years of knitting,' said Dorcas. 'I think it's even helping my arthritis!'

'It's the most powerful wool any of us has ever used,' said Jun-Yu. 'It might even be strong enough to radiate out through the town and un-knit the jumpers in people's houses.'

'It's likely to do him *some* good, whatever stitch we use,' said Dorcas.

'We've put it together with all of our Magic Wool from years past, so we'll have yards and yards,' said Jun-Yu. 'And we're working on it two at a time, in shifts, so all of our powers of concentration are gathered into it. I think we're almost there.'

There was an explosion of jingling bells followed by a bang, as the shop door swung open so quickly it hit the wall. Footsteps pounded on the stairs, and Hortense rushed into the centre of the room, her glasses askew.

'Hortense?' asked Jun-Yu, putting her knitting down. 'What on earth?'

'Jumpers!' said Hortense. 'Thousands of them!' She paused to catch her breath. 'He's back. And he's already got those machines doing something with all the wool that Will and Sophie picked.' She was holding her mobile phone. 'Should I gather the troops?'

'Immediately,' said Jun-Yu. She spoke very calmly, but she and Dorcas both began knitting so quickly, Will was surprised their needles didn't spout flames.

'This is Broadsword calling Danny Boy,' Hortense said into her phone. 'Everyone over to HQ. Repeat, everyone over to HQ.'

Dorcas giggled.

'And can we have a 10-61 here?' Hortense asked.

'What's a 10-61?' asked Will.

'That means milk for tea,' said Jun-Yu, rolling her eyes. 'Would you go and put the kettle on, Will?'

When Will got back upstairs, Jun-Yu was on her feet, measuring out the Dispelling Scarf. She was wrapping it round her hand and elbow like fallen rigging.

'I hope we'll have enough,' said Dorcas.

Hortense pulled forward a large blackboard on wheels, on which she had sketched what looked like a map of the Woolman Mill, covered with arrows, numbers, initials and exclamation points.

'Oh, goody!' said Ivy, who had just come up the stairs behind Will. 'Are we going to blow the ruddy doors off?'

'Oh, I hope so,' said Will.

'*You* aren't doing anything but going home, young man,' said Jun-Yu.

'You're joking!' said Will. 'Not again.'

'I agree with Jun-Yu,' said Matilda, who had come up the stairs with Ivy. 'It's not that we don't know you're capable, Will. You saved the day, after all.'

'Saved our bacon,' said Hortense.

'Saved our bums,' said Ivy.

'But I cannot forgive myself for how much danger we let you get into,' Jun-Yu continued, 'and I will not let it happen again.'

'We owe it to your gran,' said Matilda.

'Off with you now,' said Dorcas.

'You can ring us at bedtime if you like,' said Hortense.

Just then Holly's head bobbed up the stairwell. She was carrying the tea tray. 'Bannog, anyone? What's the plan, grans?'

Jun-Yu closed her eyes and sighed.

'No one. Under. Twenty-one. Is. On. This. Mission,' she said.

'But you need us!' said Holly. 'We don't fall for his mangy jumpers! Haven't you noticed? *We* think they're itchy and naff! So it might be an idea to have one of us along, don't you think?' Holly set the tray down and came over to Dorcas's chair. She had a shawl over her arm. 'I found your shawl at home, Gran.'

'My shawl! Thank you, dear!'

'See! We can help, we under-twenty-ones!'

'Oh, child!' said Dorcas. 'What would your mum say if she knew I'd let you get involved with such dangerous doings?'

'And what would she say if she knew *I'd* let *you*?' Holly replied, tucking the shawl around Dorcas's shoulders. 'Going after this Jasper Thingie Fitchet, with his ferrets and his factory and his—'

'Woolman!' said Dorcas, suddenly sitting upright. 'Jasper *Woolman* Fitchet.'

'What?'

'He's the Woolman boy! Now I remember!'

'Is that your Memory Shawl?' said Jun-Yu.

'Great pattern, that,' Ivy chuckled.

'Yes!' said Dorcas, raising her shawl-clad arms in the air and looking around at the circle of faces, her eyes wide. 'I remember everything!'

26

'You all know that Jasper Fitchet is from Knittington,' said Dorcas. 'What he hasn't told you is that he was born to the family that owned the mill, before they lost it all.'

'You mean the *Woolmans*?' asked Will. 'Why's he called Fitchet?'

'His mother was a Woolman,' said Dorcas. 'The last one, in fact. Oh, but they were duffers, the last of the Woolmans! Their family had run that mill for three centuries. They'd done both well and good. Set up the hospital and the almshouses and the school when they started getting rich. But then they forgot their old, careful ways, and didn't want anything to do with the factory, except for the profit.'

The grans all nodded like they knew that part.

'And then Portia Woolman married a mullocking jubber called Fitchet, who played golf and never worked a day in his life. They were always abroad, and couldn't be bothered with their little boy. He wasn't allowed to play with the local children either, because they were common.'

'I'll bet the town didn't like that,' said Hortense.

'The boy wouldn't have had any friends at all, if it hadn't been for Gertie,' said Dorcas.

'They were *friends*?' said Will.

'Thick as thieves,' said Dorcas. 'Gertie's mum was the Woolmans' cook, you see, and Gertie would come along after school. Of course, wherever Gertie went, her knitting came with her. They'd sit under the kitchen table on rainy days with their needles. Came as natural as hooting does to owls. Only thing Jasper couldn't do was Harkening Stitch. "I guess I don't have a Best Self," he would say. But Gertie never believed that.'

'Gertie always had faith,' said Jun-Yu.

'In her innocence, she taught him some powerful patterns that she shouldn't have done.'

'Well, I'll be soysed!' said Ivy.

'And told him about Magic Wool too,' said Dorcas.

'*That's* how he learnt all our tricks!' said Jun-Yu.

'Maybe he'd have been all right if things had stayed like that, and Gertie could have kept an eye on him. But Jasper got shipped off to a fancy school.'

'I'll bet he didn't fit in there either,' said Hortense.

'He'd have been neither a fox nor a hound!' said Matilda.

'What happened then?' asked Will.

'The mill failed,' Dorcas continued,

'because the family had been spending more than they earnt. Then his mum died, and his fancy school sent him packing because the fees hadn't been paid. Jasper came back to Knittington to find his dad had run off with the last of the cash.'

'Shocking!' said Matilda.

'Unspeakable!' said Jun-Yu.

'No wonder he's such a face ache,' said Ivy.

'The family house was sold, and Jasper had nowhere to go.'

'How old was he then?' asked Jun-Yu.

'About fifteen. Just Holly's age! He went to live in the empty mill, as no one wanted to buy it. He found bits of work when people took pity on him, hauling boxes in the market and doing chores. But many were unkind. Everyone had lost their jobs when the mill closed down, you see, and his father had left debts behind.'

'What about Gertie?' asked Hortense.

'She won't have let him down,' said Matilda.

'She used to bring him food. He wanted her to knit him things — wallets that were never empty, slingshots so he could take revenge, vests that would force people to give him money. But all she would make were socks for courage, and jumpers for strength, and a Combat Cardigan for ideas.'

The grans all sighed and nodded.

'Then Gertie got married.'

'Grandad!' said Will.

'That's right,' said Dorcas. 'Tom Shepherd had everything Jasper wanted: a big, loving family, proper job with work mates — he was a mechanic at the motorbike factory, with no one to cagmag him for not dressing posh — he could even knit. And then he won Gertie too.'

'Jasper must have been gutted,' said Hortense.

'He stole some of Gertie's Magic Wool, and disappeared on Tom's motorbike,' said Dorcas. 'Some say he went to Japan. Some say he went to Italy. But Gertie never forgot him. She didn't speak of it often, but it grieved her something terrible.'

'Well, knock me for six!' said Matilda.

'That's why she was always on about the rules and keeping everything top secret!' said Holly. 'She broke the rules teaching Jasper, and look what happened.'

'That would explain a lot,' said Ivy.

'So he learnt magic from Gertie, and learnt computer knitting who-knows-where, and now he's come back to take revenge on Knittington and make a fortune in the process,' said Jun-Yu.

'By making everyone desperate for his mecklekeckle jumpers,' said Hortense.

'Finally Knittington will want him,' said Matilda.

'Well, this is all very heartbreaking,' said Jun-Yu, turning to Will and Holly, 'but none of it changes the fact that this is no place for children. Even children as clever and resourceful as you two.'

'You've got as much place here right now as gravy on a sponge cake,' said Hortense.

'A rabbit on a rugby pitch,' said Matilda.

'A spider in a shoe,' said Ivy.

'Now off with you both, or I will ring your mums,' said Jun-Yu, 'and don't think I won't.'

'Are you thinking what I'm thinking?' asked Holly when they got downstairs.

'If you're thinking they're going to need us,' said Will, 'then yes.'

27

They waited in the wood behind the factory with binoculars.

'I brought my skipping rope too,' said Holly, 'in case we need to tie the creep up!'

It was a boring, anxious hour, watching nothing happen at the windows of the factory, and getting sore bums from sitting on rocks. But finally the binoculars picked up some movement. On the other side of the river, a procession of figures was heading over the footbridge from the abbey grounds.

'They're here,' said Will.

The leafy branches at the edge of the

car park shook. There was a pause, and then the grans appeared like ninjas from the trees. Faster than Will would ever have thought they could move, they scuttled towards the factory, Jun-Yu carrying a covered basket.

'Well, dress me in a cat suit and call me an Avenger,' said Holly.

'Look at them go!' said Will.

Holly and Will slid down the slope to the shrubs at the very edge of the car park, and watched through the branches. The grans had pressed themselves against the wall of the building, next to the shop door. At a sign from Jun-Yu, Hortense ducked to the other side of the door, looked in through the nearest window, and ducked back again. Then Jun-Yu began to reel out the Dispelling Scarf, the grans taking hold of it at intervals.

Will leant forward to watch. But he never did find out what the grans were about to do, because just then there was a rasping grate as a top-floor window opened, and a large white forehead appeared.

'Here comes trouble!' Holly said, sitting up straight.

'Good afternoon, ladies!' Mr Fitchet was leaning from the window.

'Mr Fitchet,' said Jun-Yu, looking up.

'I have a gift for you, ladies,' said Mr Fitchet, 'if you'll allow me.'

'We want nothing from you, Jasper,' called

Jun-Yu. 'Indeed, we've come with a gift ourselves.'

'Oh, I think you'll want these,' said Mr Fitchet.

'Not to put too fine a point on it, Fitchet,' said Hortense, 'but your gifts are about as welcome as a fly in a pie shop.'

'A bagpipe in a library,' said Matilda.

'A bus in a bluebell bed,' said Dorcas.

'A zombie in a crèche,' said Ivy.

'And if you'll just sit tight for a moment . . .' Jun-Yu said. She began unreeling the Dispelling Scarf again, going twice as quickly as before, and taking giant steps along the side of the building.

Just then something pink and fluffy floated down from the window, like candy floss on a breeze, and landed in the middle of the circle of grans. Jun-Yu didn't finish her sentence. Instead all of the grans sighed at once, as if they were at a school concert and their grandchildren were singing in the chorus.

'Oooooh! Looooook!' They surged forward, dropping the Dispelling Scarf to grasp at the pink thing, stretching it out in the air between them.

'Lovely!' said Ivy.

'Exquisite!' said Matilda.

Fitchet disappeared for a moment and then appeared at the window again, his arms full of something.

'*Oh, pants!*' said Will.

'Cardigans, actually,' said Holly.

The cardigans swirled down through the air. For a second they lay on the ground, like fallen rose petals, and then the grans fell forward to gather them up in their arms.

'Sound action stations!' said Holly.

'We shall beat to—'

Thump.

Sophie came sliding down the slope, banging into Will's back.

'*Not again!*' said Will.

'I followed you,' said Sophie.

'Look, Sophie, I don't care *what* Cronk

said,' Will fumed. 'I don't want you anywhere near that troll!' He looked at Holly. 'Holly, please, please just stay here and don't let her go any closer!'

Without waiting for an answer, he pushed through the branches and pounded across the tarmac. 'Stop!' he called out to the grans. 'Don't! Jun-Yu, Matilda! Don't put them on!'

But they already were. Each of the grans had put first one arm, then another into a cardigan. They murmured in awe as they did up the buttons.

'I've never seen such beauty!' said Hortense.

'Look at the work in that!' said Dorcas.

The cardigans were the colour of fruit jellies, flecked with black, and each one had a patch stuck on it: goggle-eyed butterflies, squat goofy kittens, bratty-looking fairies. Even Sophie wouldn't be caught dead in these. But the grans were spinning round, admiring one another and exclaiming. Their old Combat Cardigans were no match for the powerful new wool.

'Can't you see what he's doing?' Will shouted.

'Don't be rude, Will,' said Jun-Yu. 'Mr Fitchet has gone out of his way to make us something really special, and I, for one, am simply overcome!'

The door to the shop opened and Fitchet came out, his blue eyes sparkling and his pressed lips grinning.

'Mr Fitchet, we don't know how to thank you!' said Jun-Yu.

'If you really want to thank me, dear lady,' said Fitchet, holding the door open wide, 'you can come in and buy more of my new collection.'

'No!' Will's heart skipped three beats and then galloped forward. 'Don't go in there!' Will was about to rush at Jun-Yu, to try to yank the cardigan off her, when Jasper turned towards him, his eyes like bullets.

'I have a new children's collection too.

Much better than my earlier models. Much more *effective*.'

Jun-Yu had already walked into the building, and all the other grans were following her. Will scooped up the Dispelling Scarf, and, stuffing it into the basket, ran in after them.

28

Jasper Fitchet pulled the big wooden doors shut behind them, securing them with an iron bar that clanged as it fell into place. Will swallowed. Well, at least that would keep Sophie safe: Holly would have come running in after her gran in another two seconds, and Sophie would have been right behind her.

'Now, ladies!' said Fitchet, his grin widening, and his bright blue eyes shining. 'Allow me to show you to our dressing rooms. Perhaps you'd like to take your bulky cardigans off and enjoy the elegant fit of your new gifts properly.'

'Oooh, lovely, yes!' The grans all surged

towards the velvet curtains, and a second later five Combat Cardigans flumped to the floor.

Fitchet made a clicking sound with his mouth and five ferrets came running along the floor. They scurried to the dressing rooms, each one taking a cardigan in its teeth and dragging it away from the grans.

Will ran towards the dressing rooms, then ran towards the ferrets, then ran back towards the dressing rooms.

'No! Stop! Don't!' he shouted.

'Here we go gathering jumpers today,' Mr Fitchet said in a sing-song voice.

The velvet curtains opened again and one by one the grans rushed to the big mirrors, each stepping in front of the others to get a better look.

'Gorgeous!'

'Though you've got to admit, mine's the best.'

'I think that would look better on me, actually.'

'I want them all!' said Jun-Yu.

Mr Fitchet chuckled. 'Even the Knittery Knitting Knot wants me now.' He opened his arms. 'No need to fight, ladies!' he said. 'There are oodles of clothes here. Enough for everyone. Please make yourselves at home!'

'Ooooh!'

'Don't mind if I do!'

Suddenly, the man whirled around to face Will.

'But I almost forgot. My new children's collection.'

Will wasn't fast enough. Before he could run, or even look away, Jasper had lifted a jumper out of an open drawer, and set it down with a swirl on the counter top in front of Will.

Will froze. It was a copy of the magic jumper. Only instead of the dense, soft wool, this jumper was made of something prickly. Where the magic jumper was navy blue, battleship grey and racing green, this jumper was turquoise, brown and lime. There was no stripe of sparkly gold; instead there were tiny flecks of black dotted over the whole thing.

As ugly as it was, Will couldn't stop looking at it. He managed to turn his head away, but his eyes stayed stuck to the jumper. The longer he looked, the more he found he wanted to touch it. It was like looking at chocolate – the more you look, the more you want to eat it.

He wanted to put the jumper on.

'There you are, Will. Give it a try, why don't you? It's for you.'

Will knew he shouldn't. He knew it was dangerous. But he wanted to. He hugged his magic jumper to him, the jumper Gran had made, trying to make his mind quiet. And suddenly it was as if she was there. Her soft, wrinkled hand was smoothing his forehead, like it used to do when he'd been sick with a fever. Gently, like a warm feather, the invisible hand cupped his eyes, smoothing them downwards, until he was able to close his eyelids against the black-flecked jumper. For just a second he felt the silence.

And then he knew what he had to do.

He opened his eyes.

'I'll put yours on if you put mine on,' he said, and he pulled one of his arms out of the magic jumper.

'Ha,' said Fitchet. 'Do you think I can't recognize your gran's knitting?'

'*I'm* wearing it, and it isn't hurting *me*,' said Will. He pulled his other arm out of its sleeve.

'Well, she probably made it just for you, to give you extra powers. Probably does the opposite on anyone else. I know all about her ways, you know.'

Will was about to answer when he noticed Fitchet's face change. He was looking at the dangling sleeve of the jumper, and his eyes seemed to go . . . soft. The tight little grin became a small, squidgy O.

Jasper Fitchet was staring at the little embroidered bee on the wrist.

That was when Will realized. It wasn't a bee at all – it was a wasp. *Jasper* was an old word for a wasp – a farm word, a village word, a Dorcas-and-Gran word.

'You *recognize* it, don't you?' said Will. 'She didn't make it for me at all. She made it for *you*!'

Fitchet looked at Will, looked at the jumper.

'She made it to help you with Harkening Stitch. Right before she died.'

'She made that to *help* me?' asked Fitchet slowly. 'She still thought I could . . .'

Taking a deep breath, Will pulled the magic jumper off over his head and put it on the counter next to the other jumper. He swallowed. It was like taking off a life preserver.

'Just touch it if you don't believe me,' he said, trying to smile.

Very slowly, Jasper reached out and touched the magic jumper. His bright eyes widened.

'Look,' said Will. 'I'll put an arm in yours

232

if you put an arm in mine. That's how sure I am.'

He took a step forward, handed the magic jumper to Jasper Fitchet with his left hand, and took the Fitchet & Ferret jumper with his right. Slowly he put one arm into the sleeve. It felt like putting his arm into a snake.

Fitchet put an arm into the magic jumper. He sighed.

Will put his other arm into the Fitchet & Ferret jumper. Now both of his arms were in snakes.

Fitchet put his other arm into the magic jumper. The wolf-tail eyebrows unknitted and moved gently apart.

Slowly, Will put the Fitchet & Ferret jumper over his head. At first it was like falling into soup — everything felt slow and warm and thick around him. Then suddenly he was breathless. It was like when he and Ben started laughing at something silly and couldn't stop. His heart rushed as if he'd eaten too many sweets.

Meanwhile, Jasper was wearing the magic jumper, and he was staring at Will. *He's all right*, Will found himself thinking. *I don't know what we were on about.* But Jasper was gasping, his blue eyes round.

'What have I done?' he said. 'Take it off, boy, take it off!'

But Will didn't know what Mr Fitchet was so upset about. 'No, hey, it's fine!' he laughed. 'It's good. It's great. It's no problem.'

Jasper's eyes were wide. He looked around the room wildly, then back at Will.

'Will. You must, you *must* take that jumper off. Please listen to me. In the name of your gran, please believe me.'

Even thinking about taking off the jumper hurt. Will didn't want to. The jumper felt like sunlight in February. It felt like a whole stadium shouting together as his own team scored. It felt like his last piece of chocolate. It felt like winning.

Fitchet rushed over to a drawer in the wall. It opened with a low, rumbling roll, and there inside it were the stolen mittens. The man plucked one from the drawer and darted back to Will. Taking Will's hand, he slid the mitten on to it, holding it there so Will couldn't take it off.

Once, in a rugby game last winter, someone had kicked Will in the head by accident, and he'd fallen unconscious on to the field. When he came to, he saw faces around him in the air. The mouths were moving, but the voices seemed to be coming from far away. It took a long time before he started understanding what they were saying. That's what he felt like now.

He looked down at his hand and saw the mitten, and then he remembered everything. It was like turning off the telly after many hours, and in the silence, finally thinking a thought of his own again. Like he'd jumped into a cool lake on a sticky, sleepy day.

Will ripped off the Fitchet & Ferret jumper and dropped it on the floor, the mitten tumbling down with it. He felt a jolt of pain.

His whole torso was coming awake with pins and needles. He was freezing cold, empty with hunger and *desperately* sad. He wanted to be home, he wanted Gran, he wanted to put the Fitchet & Ferret jumper back on. He thrust his arm out towards it. Anything to make the awful feeling stop.

Jasper kicked the Fitchet & Ferret jumper across the floor and dived on the fallen mitten. A second later he had the mitten over Will's hand again, holding it on, and staring into Will's face. Tears were leaking from the man's eyes, down on to the magic jumper.

'Are you all right, Will?'

Will shuddered, but then the pins and needles ebbed, and his hands felt warm again. He could see, he could hear, and there was quiet. He took a slow breath.

'What have I done?' whispered Jasper. He looked out at the grans, now shoving one another to get in front of the biggest mirror.

'Mr Fi-i-tchet!' called Hortense.

'We LOVE your collection!' said Jun-Yu.

'We want to buy everything!' cried Matilda.

'Come and take our money!' cried Ivy.

'What should I do?' Mr Fitchet whispered.

Wsh-skat, wsh-skat.

What was that sound? It was coming from down in the car park.

Wsh-skat, wsh-skat.

A small voice started singing.

'In through the rabbit hole,
Round the big tree,
Up comes the rabbit,
And off goes she!'

It was Sophie, singing the knit-and-purl rhyme while she and Holly turned the skipping rope.

'Under the fence,
Grab that sheep,
Out of the fence
And off we leap!'

Brilliant Holly! All at once Will realized what needed to happen.

'Do some Harkening Stitch!' he told Jasper. 'It will fix everything. Here . . .' He swept the basket up off the floor, and pulled out the Dispelling Scarf, the end that was still attached to a ball of yarn with needles sticking out of it. 'Just a few stitches, at the end here.'

'B-b-but – I can't,' said Jasper. 'I never could. My Best Self . . . isn't very good.'

'Gran thought it was. That's why she made that jumper.'

'She made me something every year,' said Jasper. 'Every single year she sent me something. Japan, Italy, Germany, she always found me.'

'See?' said Will. 'She believed in you!'

'But I never put one of them on! I thought she was trying to hurt me. I thought she must be angry with me. I'd betrayed her, after all. I'd,' he swallowed, 'I'd stolen from her. Why would *anyone* want to help me? I unravelled every jumper she sent; every scarf and every glove, to get the Magic Wool out. And all this time . . .' He put his hands over his face.

'If you didn't have a Best Self, you wouldn't be feeling bad right now,' Will pointed out. He handed Jasper the knitting needles and the end of the Dispelling Scarf. 'Put all your other thoughts down,' said Will, 'so there's nothing in your head but the sound of the river, and the sound of that song.'

'Gather from the hedges,
Golden in the dawn,
Wash it in the river,
Spread it on the lawn.'

Will glanced over Mr Fitchet's shoulder, towards the windows. He could see Holly and Sophie sweeping the rope around in fast, round circles, and children running from every direction, jumping through them. There were Olive and Annie, Lorelei and Simone, Ivan and Alexi, and Ruby and Ben. Some of them began to pick up the words to the song, so the singing got louder each minute:

'*Card it with a carding comb,*
Careful as you can,
Spin it with a spindle,
And give it to your gran.'

Suddenly Harkening Stitch sounded like the best fun ever.

Jasper sat down on one of the elegant sofas and began to knit, silently mouthing the words of the song, his white eyebrows dancing up and down as his fingers tugged and cajoled and wrapped. After a moment he looked up.

'I'm-I'm doing it!' he said.

'Keep going,' said Will.

Five centimetres of knitting grew from between the needles, then ten. First he smiled, a proper wide smile, like his face unfolding. Then he laughed, and instead of the reedy oboe, it sounded like bagpipes and brass.

'I'm doing it!' said Jasper. 'Oh, Will! I've done it!'

There was a sound of car tyres on loose gravel below.

'Bandits! Bandits!' called Holly's voice. 'Car park!'

'Keep going,' said Will. 'Just keep going.'

But the song had stopped. Car doors closed outside. Jasper looked up, his face wrinkled in doubt.

Will touched his hand. '*Card it with a carding comb, careful as you can . . .*'

Jasper kept knitting. '*Spin it with a spindle,*' he whispered, '*and give it to your gran.*'

Will went to the window. Out on the tarmac two black cars were parked alongside the building. The children had scattered, except for Holly, who stood at the furthest edge of the car park, holding Sophie close. Four men in dark suits were walking from the cars towards the factory. All along the side of the building, the grans thrust their heads out of the windows.

'KNITWITCH!' one of them shouted.

Fitchet shot to his feet.

'KNITWITCH! The Knitwitch!' The grans pulled their heads back into the shop. Like starlings at roosting time, they ran from one end of the shop to the other. Will couldn't tell whether they were excited or frightened. Finally they plunged into the dressing rooms, yanking the velvet curtains shut behind them.

But it was clear that Jasper Fitchet was terrified. His face turned white and his eyes went wide as empty windows. His hands fell to his sides and the knitting needles clattered to the floor.

Something scraped at the old oak door. *Scritch. Scritch.* It sounded like sharp claws. *Let me in*, it seemed to say.

Then there was a loud knock at the double doors.

Jasper began to sway.

Something shot up into the crack between the doors, knocking the iron bar out of its hooks. It sounded like a single church bell as it crashed to the floor.

Scritch. Scritch. Waving lines of dizziness

rushed across Will's eyes.

The double doors swung slowly open, and Mr Fitchet fell like a tree. Will ran to him and caught his head just before it crashed to the floor. Jasper had fainted, his hand still clutching the knitted scarf.

A corgi trotted into the room, and then another one, and a third. They were followed by two broad-shouldered men in dark suits, with curly wires stuck into their ears. They walked sideways into the room and all around the edges, looking up and down along the walls, and out of the windows. They nodded at each other. One of them touched the wire in his ear and said, 'Green.'

Then they stood at either side of the door like two giant statues, their eyes roving.

Will stood up, his heart pounding.

A small gran he'd never met stepped into the shop, wearing a quilted rain jacket and a silk scarf knotted under her chin. She walked with soft, clipping steps to Mr Fitchet, and bent to take the end of the knitted scarf out of his hands. She peered at it for a moment, examining the Dispelling Stitch, and then the Harkening Stitch that was added on at the end. Then she took the needles in her hands, and added one final stitch. With a flick of her wrist she flung the Dispelling Scarf so it landed in a circle on the floor, surrounding the fainted form of Jasper Fitchet.

There was a gentle rustling all over the building, as if thousands of knots were untying themselves and falling loose to the floor. When it finally stopped, the air was filled with sparkling gold flecks. A breeze rushed through the factory, and soon the golden sparkles were floating like snowflakes up into the sky around the building, settling in the trees, scurrying across the car park, and spinning along the surface of the river like glittering petals.

The grans came tumbling out of the dressing rooms, dressed in their own clothes again. They stood still for a second, their eyes wide. Then, all at once, they curtseyed.

It was surprisingly graceful.

One of the men in dark suits came up the spiral staircase from the basement. He was carrying two sacks under his arms. Fluffy strands of fleece poked out of the tops, the colour of walnut coffee cake, glinting with gold. He held one of them out to Jun-Yu. Her mouth dropped open for a second, before she pulled herself up and took the sack in her arms with a gracious tilt of her head.

The gran in the quilted jacket looked at Jun-Yu with a small smile and a deep nod. Then she turned to Will, looked him up and down as if sizing him up, and gave a short, satisfied bob of her head.

'Carry on,' she said to the room at large.

The corgis followed her out.

Jasper suddenly came to. 'Was that—? Was that—?'

'That was the Knitwitch, you nitwit,' said Ivy.

'Head of the Commonwealth, Defender of the Faith,' said Hortense.

'Duchess of Edinburgh, Duke of Normandy,' said Matilda.

'The Uber Gran,' said Ivy.

'The Lord of Man,' said Dorcas.

'Her Majesty, the Queen,' said Jun-Yu.

29

All over Knittington, jumpers had unravelled. In rooms across town, the Magic Wool had freed itself, and some of it was still sticking to the trees as Will walked through the back garden two weeks later.

'Hey, Will!' said Rosie next door. 'Want to see a striped dahlia?'

'Sorry! Can't stop,' said Will.

The Pingles were rebuilding their shed, after they'd had an accident on Wednesday, trying to make Greek fire.

'Hey, Will,' said Alex. 'Want to see the new TARDIS? Plenty of room for the jousting kit now!'

'Another time!' said Will, unlatching the gate and slipping through.

'Like to help fill the bird feeders, Will?' Miss Violet called from across the alley. 'I've got the new autumn seed mix.'

'Not just now, thanks, but I bet Sophie will.'

'We've got a new pogo stick, Will!' said Olive, her head bobbing up over the top of the fence.

'So all three of us can bounce at once!' said Annie. They were bobbing in time with the drums and fiddles in the morris dancers' garden.

'Sorry! Gotta run!'

He was off to The Knittery, for the first meeting of the Gang of Grans since they had been made an official Knitwork Knot.

Holly was at the till when Will arrived, putting skeins of extra-chunky purple yarn into a bag for an excited lady with brand-new knitting needles.

'Thank you!' Holly said with a smile. 'Come

back soon and let us know how you get on with the project!'

The door closed with a jingle of bells.

'Quick!' said Holly, her smile sliding off. 'Turn that sign around for me, will you? It's been heaving in here all day and I'm *desperate* to—'

'Is that Will down there?' called a voice from upstairs.

'Yes, that's me!' said Will, turning the sign on the front door so it said CLOSED. He went up the winding stairs.

The grans were all sitting knitting round a table full of scarves and hats and shawls. People recovered from the Fitchet & Ferret jumpers more quickly when they put on some proper magical knitting, and donations had been sent from all over the Knitwork. With the help of Mr Fitchet's ferrets, the grans had distributed them to nearly every sufferer in Knittington.

Jasper Fitchet was at the table too. The Rogue Knitter was finally working on his

Harkening Jumper.

'Did you notice,' Hortense was asking, 'that those security people were wearing Harkening Vests under their dark suits?'

'I wonder if Her Majesty wears a Harkening Jumper?' asked Matilda.

'Her Majesty doesn't need a Harkening Jumper,' said Dorcas. 'Her Majesty *is* a Harkening Jumper.'

'I've heard she has Harkening Pants,' said Ivy.

Jun-Yu gave her a Paddington Hard Stare. 'Ivy,' she said. 'We do *not* speak of the Royal scanties.'

Holly came up the stairs. Instead of sitting at the table, she lay down on the rug with her arms above her head.

'I'm knackered!' she said.

'Cream crackered!' said Ivy.

'I'm not sure the shop has ever had a busier day,' said Jun-Yu. 'I'm a bit fatigued myself.'

'Clapped out and whacked,' said Matilda.

'Mullered and chin-strapped,' said Hortense.

'Wappered, daggered, and bathered out,' said Dorcas.

Even Will had been running all over town, putting scarves and hats through letter boxes.

'I hope you'll allow me to make us all some tea!' said Mr Fitchet, shooting up from his seat. 'I'd be only too happy.' He seemed to have a hard time saying he was sorry out loud, but he was always carrying boxes and opening doors and giving Dorcas lifts into the shop. He was still neatly dressed in tweeds and a tie, but there was something less stiff about his collar, and he was wearing the jumper Gran had made.

'Now,' said Jun-Yu, as soon as he'd gone down the stairs. 'Are we all in agreement?' She looked around the circle, and everyone nodded.

'He's an annoying little ferret,' said Ivy, 'but I guess he's *our* annoying little ferret.'

'Will and Holly? Are you all right with this?'

'Oh, do we count now?' asked Holly, sitting up and smiling her crooked smile.

'You are now a junior member of the Knittington Knittery Knitting Knot,' said Jun-Yu, 'and so will you be, Will, as soon as you've finished your Harkening Jumper.' They had decided to fast-track Will to the Harkening stage, because he knew so much about magic knitting already. 'So you both have a vote.'

They were all in agreement.

When Jasper came rattling up the stairs with a tray of tea and cake, Jun-Yu told him to put the tray down. 'Jasper. I'm pleased to tell you that you have been accepted as a probationary member of the Knittington Knittery Knitting Knot, contingent upon your completion of a Harkening Jumper, a Combat Cardigan, and twelve community service knitting projects, to be overseen by the afore-mentioned knot,' she coughed, 'which is to say, us.'

'Furthermore,' Jun-Yu continued, 'we are appointing you official Keeper of the Kit — which is to say, the carding combs and —

spindles – and presenting you with this hat of office.'

The hat was shaped like a bowler hat, except that – of course – it was knitted with multi-coloured stripes. Jun-Yu handed it to Jasper, who smiled so widely that Will wondered if his face would fold in on itself. The grans had figured that having a badge of office would make Jasper so happy he would stay loyal to the Knitwork ideals, and it looked like they were right. It wouldn't hurt that the hat was laced through with an honesty stitch.

'I – I – thank you – I don't know what to say.' He was beaming.

'Don't say anything,' said Holly. 'Just pour the tea.'

'Now,' said Jun-Yu, as they settled down with slices of raisin rum fruit cake (Jasper's speciality), 'shall I read this Knitwork email out, before it self-destructs?'

The grans all clapped their hands and stamped.

'Firstly, we are congratulated on the acceptance of our own invented pattern, hereafter known as Dispelling Stitch, into the Knitwork Pattern Book. It is considered a Class A, or Highly Useful pattern.'

The grans all cheered, and Dorcas looked especially smug.

It had turned out that inventing their own pattern was one of the requirements to becoming a Knitwork Knot, or renewing membership after the loss of a leader. The grans were also planning to submit the Seven-League Slippers for a Knitwork award, as soon as they had reknitted them.

'Secondly, we are highly commended for continuing Gertie's research into the production of Magic Wool on the Isle of Man. We are requested to continue our experiments to see if we can reproduce this year's results again next year.'

'Oh! We could go to the Classic TT!' said Ivy.

'Ahem,' said Jun-Yu. 'Apparently, while

they knew about how to gather the wool, they *hadn't* known that the wool might become more powerful when children pick it. They speculate it's because children make it into a game, and that the fun helps the wool.'

Here Holly chuckled and looked smug.

'They're also interested to note that *our* Manx wool was even better than Gertie's! They think it has to do with the sheep running wild and eating native plants.'

'Just like Cronk's sister said!' Now it was Will's turn to look smug.

'Finally, we are invited to send a representative to Scotland next year to help harvest Magic Fleece from the Knitwork's ancient herds.'

And here *everyone* looked smug.

'To the Knittington Knittery Knitting Knot!' said Jasper.

They all raised their cups.

30

It was strange going back to school. Everyone had been somewhere, even if it was only camping in their nan's back garden. Robyn and Isabelle, Annie and Olive, Clara and Marius, and Finn and Vivien had all been to Cornwall. Ben had been spelunking in Wales. Rafi and his brothers had all gone to India, and Henry and Jacob had been to Maine. Colin had gone to Ireland in a camper van, and Ruby had gone to circus school. Will wanted to tell them about the Isle of Man and being on a motorbike and what it felt like to wake up in the middle of the night with ferrets in his room. But all he could actually say was, 'My gran died and I learnt to knit.'

'You learnt to *knit*?' said Colin.

'Sailors knit,' said Will. 'And my grandad used to knit. So what? It's fun.'

Colin started calling him Granny, but Will just laughed. Funny. Last year he probably would have called Colin something back, and they'd have spent the whole maths lesson shooting rubber bands at each other. But now he didn't care. His gran had been amazing, after all. Almost a spy. Almost a witch – the good kind, of course.

Colin tried to get Rafi to laugh along, but Rafi just said, 'Hey, don't knock it till you've tried it!' He shot Will a glance, and Will could tell he was remembering a certain skipping rope.

But it was fine to get back to being normal, really – just going to school and playing football in the road and trying to figure out how to make his bike go faster. Of course, 'normal' was better than it used to be, now.

Jasper Fitchet had turned his factory into a school for crafts and mechanics, and, thanks to an idea Mum had while wearing her patchwork jumper, she had a new job teaching there. There was a giant kitchen in the factory now, too. Ben's dad hired it twice a week to use the huge mixers and colossal baking trays for his new cake business (Ben's Bakes), and sometimes Will and Ben got to help. Will and Sophie would go the factory after school and play at the river, or run up and down the spiral staircases, or help in the café (where the cake was Ben's dad's, of course).

Dad was happier too. He'd managed to write two lectures and an article since Will had given him the green-bean hat. Dad swore by it and called it his Thinking Cap.

Even the ferrets were happier, now that they lived at the farm park.

But more than that, normal was better now that Will knew his little sister could tame giant dogs and escape from kidnappers; that charity shops might be full of magic mittens;

that their babysitter had a magic skipping rope; that any old lady might turn out to be a motorbiking crusader against evil; and that he, himself, could save the day.

'Never judge a book by its cover,' said Matilda.

'Don't judge a chair by its chintz,' said Dorcas.

'You can't measure the sea with a teacup,' said Jun-Yu.

'All that twitters is not a twit,' said Ivy.

'You just never know,' said Hortense.

No, thought Will. *You really don't.*

My Thanks To:

Chicken House, Pickled Ink, and the Bath Spa University MA program in Creative Writing For Young People.

All of the staff at the Corinium Museum, for their patience.

My writing group (the Bradies) for helping and hoping.

Lucy, for bringing the flowers, every time.

Lizzie, Athena, Beth and Christina, for being so certain.

The Barings, Byrnes and Brichoux; Cannocks, Kellums, and Keiners; Harrises, Hambrooks, and Llywds; Mac-Oois and Olsons; Pringle-Cadles and Pritchard-Cuomos; Ryder-Walkers and Shellen-bergers; Linsey-Woolsey and the Textilians, and the New Brewery Crew, for their dear selves.

Jo and Finn, for knitting lessons.

EHE, for tending the wounded.

Lierre, for sharing.

The Knitwitch herself, for putting up with such terrible liberties.

And Tim, for taking me pillion.

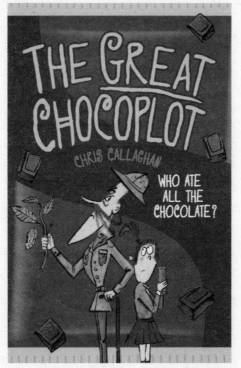

THE GREAT CHOCOPLOT by CHRIS CALLAGHAN

It's the end of chocolate – for good! A chocolate mystery . . . At least that's what they're saying on TV.

Jelly and her gran are gobsmacked – they love a Blocka Choca bar or two.

But then a trail of clues leads back to a posh chocolate shop in town owned by the distinctly bitter Garibaldi Chocolati.

Is it really the chocopocalypse, or a chocoplot to be cracked?

With an excellent cast of characters, laugh-out-loud moments, and witty and sharp observations, this is a great choice for fans of Dahl and Walliams.
GUARDIAN

Paperback, ISBN 978-1-910002-51-3, £6.99 • ebook, ISBN 978 -1-910655-57-3, £6.99